SEARCH AND RESCUE

DAVID NUTT

Copyright © 2019 David Nutt

David Nutt asserts his moral right to be identified as the author of this work.

All rights reserved. No part of this publication may be produced or transmitted in any form or by any means, electronic or mechanical, including photocopying, recording or information storage and retrieval systems, without permission in writing from the copyright holder.

Published by Plum Tree Publishing

Author contact: nuttd3907@gmail.com

This is a work of fiction. Names, characters, places and incidents either are the product of the author's imagination or are used fictitiously, and any resemblance to actual persons, living or dead, events or locales is entirely coincidental.

A catalogue record for this book is available from the National Library of New Zealand.

Thanks to Martin Taylor who provided the encouragement, kindness and professionalism to bring this book to its final form.

To My Parents

CONTENTS

The Voice	1
Facial Securities	9
The Morning Glow	17
The Romancer	25
The Ormsby Translation	31
Gabrielle	39
Evening Song	43
The Great Jo Lee	51
Sand	59
Footnotes to Plato	67
The Key	77
Dipa's Demon	83
Not High Enough	91
Modern Painters	99
Chalk	107
The Yellow and the Green	113
The Spinney	115
The Masterclass	123
The Tent	135
In Transit	143
The Mentor	151
The Hit	159
At Least It Was a Job	167
Talent and Confidence	175
The Lake Poets	183
The Lady with the Laptop	191
Henry	199
The Judgement of Paris	207
Happiness	215
Heaven	221
The Interview	227

Twenty Eighty-four   235

About the Author   243

THE VOICE

"It's that voice, the voice in your head. It's always there chatting away, original, charming, humble. It's only a question of listening to it and then you can find yourself."

Barton often made strange statements of this kind which had little relevance to what they were supposed to be studying. The few students who were actually listening to him didn't mind. They liked that he treated them as equals.

The classroom door opened. There had been no knocking. The school secretary was standing in the room, asking for him to come outside with her.

"It's your wife; you must go to the hospital immediately."

Barton understood, but he found he couldn't rouse himself out of his teaching mode.

"But my class," he said.

"Don't worry about that. We'll see to it."

"Of course," he answered, gathering himself together.

"Good luck," she called to his retreating figure.

He doesn't want to go, she thought to herself as he disappeared from view. Despite his impressive physical appearance, she had always seen his inadequacies. On the whole she admired the teachers at the school for their hard work and dedication to a difficult job, but Barton was an exception. He seemed to try hard, but no one found him at all convincing. As far as she could tell there was nothing there, no 'punch' was the way she put it to herself. Everyone felt sorry for him, even the kids. She wondered if there was any fate worse than being universally pitied? Probably, she replied to her own thought as she entered the classroom, which was even noisier than when Barton was there supposedly teaching them English Literature.

IT WAS TRUE, he didn't want to go to the hospital. He had always recoiled from any major event. He liked calm and quietness best of all. Ordinary, dull times when he could be peaceful and drift into the musing state he longed for; those times when he was barely aware of himself and certainly not the centre of anyone else's attention.

He knew the bypass would be blocked at this time of day, but he took it anyway. He wanted to be late. He detested the idea of being thrust into the limelight.

He need not have worried; by the time he got there it was long over. His son had been born. His mother-in-law had taken charge and he had only to perform the background, bit part he wanted to play. They had not expected him to be any sooner; in all the rush it had been some time before anyone thought of contacting him.

It was still a test, quite a drama. His wife lay low in the bed; the bravery with which she smiled at him made his heart die, simply die away. He knew he did not deserve such a dear, courageous woman. He was so grateful that she did not pretend to believe in him; she had never expected greatness or even competence, she just accepted him and loved him. He could feel her love gripping him, folding him to her. He would have gladly loved her in return, but he did not think himself capable of it. He believed that only brave, selfless people can love, the rest just get lost in themselves, in their own debris.

The baby was wrapped tightly and lying in a cradle, looking puzzled and somewhat put out, like someone who has been woken up in the middle of the night. Somebody said that he had been checked over and was perfect.

Barton could not believe that he had had anything to do with that. It was biology, not him, not the inept individual who had taken up residence in his handsome body. He agonised endlessly about how separate he felt from his physical being and whether everyone else felt the same partition. He had always been good looking, very tall with a craggy face, imposing shoulders and intelligent brown eyes that seemed to see everything. This was how he survived his trial of a job; had he been less physically imposing he knew that what little authority he had with his teenage students would have vanished and that he would have gone under completely. As it was, they let him drone away in front of them and seemed to accept his right to be there. His mother-in-law was someone else who was taken in by how he appeared. She was a tough, smart woman, the sort who would despise any weakness in a man, but he so much looked the part that she had never shown him anything but respect. Indeed, she liked him and listened to his opinions, not that she was ever influenced by them. Barton liked to think he had good, sensible ideas, but no one ever took them seriously. He was always written off as an academic dreamer in his ivory tower, a man totally divorced from the practical business of organising his family life.

His mother-in-law, smiling, picked up his son and put the boy into Barton's powerful arms. The baby was not much larger than one of Barton's wide hands. He raised his eyes to his wife who was watching him lovingly. There was no weight; the child seemed to weigh nothing at all. For once in his life, just for those few moments, Barton was not self-conscious and did not notice who was observing him. It was a moment of something he did not recognise and only later, after much thought, had he understood that it was joy. This was what joy felt like. It was an actual feeling and not merely a concept. The moment felt so liberating.

We live for such a long time, said the quiet voice in his head, *such a very long time.*

The boy was looking up at him. He still looked puzzled but pleased also.

"Let them rest," his mother-in-law said, taking the child back and laying it down. She seemed to be implying that Barton should leave. He had told her how he intended to arrange things for the following day and how he had prepared everything that was necessary. His mother-in-law had her own plans, which she used to overrule his.

In less than an hour, he was back in his hatchback heading to his empty home. When he had left, his wife had looked at him imploringly and a nurse had told him he could stay if he wanted to. He had left anyway, filled with a nervous desperation to get away.

Locked once again into the bypass traffic jam, he remembered that his cellphone was still switched off. It always was during his classes; this was why they had had to ring the school. There were three missed calls. His wife, his mother-in-law and just a few moments before, his brother had called him. He should call him back when he got home. His brother would invite him to dinner. He didn't want that but would find it impossible to refuse once they were talking on the phone, and so Barton switched the phone off again. This seemed extreme even to him, but Barton wanted to be alone. He wanted to think. Only by thinking could he make the day real. This may not be understandable to most people but that was how it was for him, and he felt he had the right, for once, to assert himself.

Until he saw the sign, the idea of stopping at the casino had never occurred to him. The place held no special attraction for him, but this was a big day, a huge day. He wanted something special. Fish fingers at home would hardly do it, and his brother's family were such difficult people. They were kind, of course they were, but they lived on a different planet, one that he could never learn the language of. His unworldliness and his ignorance about sport and TV shows always made them laugh at him. Friendly laughter, but it was not the way he wanted to spend this special evening.

He pulled into the casino car park which was almost empty, it being late afternoon on a week day. There were two smartly dressed bouncers either side of the door. Barton nodded to them, which seemed the right thing to do. There was no entry fee, all he had to do was open the heavy wooden doors.

He was surprised that there was no barrier or reception or anything; he could simply walk into the unexpectedly beautiful gaming room. For nearly a hundred years the building had been the main branch of a major bank. There were tall marble columns and a huge domed ceiling. It seemed to Barton more like one of Wren's smaller churches than a gaming hall. The tables were overseen by a selection of men and women, all in a standard uniform of black trousers, purple waistcoats, white shirts and small purple bow ties. The croupiers, standing at empty tables, were looking not only bored but faintly hostile. No one in the room showed any display of good humour; the atmosphere was dour and resentful.

Barton wondered what to do next. If he bought chips and gambled, then surely that would be dangerous. He might win of course, but given the way casinos are set up he was much more likely to lose and what sort of omen would that be for his newborn son? On the other hand, if he was not going to gamble, what was he going to do? No one took any notice of him. There was a bar. Barton realised that this was surely the very thing. He enjoyed wine, he liked full-bodied reds and, to his delight, he saw on the shelf behind the counter a bottle of Zinfandel.

The first glass disappeared with amazing speed. He was feeling thirsty and hungry as well as euphoric, and the wine somehow answered each of these sensations perfectly. He ordered a second glass and that was when she emerged at his side, a woman in a cocktail dress which appeared to be silk and was the colour of rubies. The dress bothered him; it seemed utterly out of place at this time of day in what was clearly a place of business. She had short blonde hair and a pretty face, which was made up to make her look inhumanly perfect, like a doll.

She nodded at him and asked, "Had a good day?"

Politeness demanded he answer. "Extremely good, thank you. My child, my son was born today." He was surprised at the confidence in his voice. She was the first person he had told and the telling of it made it more true.

"In that case you should buy me a drink," she answered, smiling, but the smile was false and insincere.

He hated that bitter smile. It was sarcastic. He felt it demeaned them both. For a moment he couldn't remember where he had seen it before but then realised that it was the sort of smile some of his thirteen-year-old students gave him. He saw dozens of such smiles every day.

"Of course," he answered, "whatever you like."

She nodded to the barman, who knew what to provide. It was a double whisky.

"So," she said after taking her first sip, "you're free for the night?" She looked at him with a questioning expression. He rehearsed in his mind the countless phrases he had heard used in this situation during the hundreds of times he had seen this scene dramatised. He held his wine glass halfway to his lips while his mind drifted. This woman seemed too young and fresh to be picking up men in bars and yet he supposed there were big rewards to be had. Perhaps she was desperate for money or just too dead in spirit to care what she did. As happened so often with Barton, what he actually said was far removed from what he was thinking.

"I wonder," he began, "do you ever hear a voice in your head that seems to be talking beyond what is going on around you? It tells you everything that is important but is so soft that you can barely hear it. It's always so smart, yet humble, never demanding or imposing anything on you."

The woman was not at all surprised by this question and seemed to think it was some sort of game.

"Wow," she answered, "that's heavy. Well, I suppose everyone talks to themselves sometimes, but that's not what you mean, is it. No, to be honest, no and I'm glad I don't hear voices. Isn't that one of the symptoms of schizophrenia?"

She was not upset by this 'game', indeed she was attracted by it. He was being respectful towards her and seemed to care what she said. He was certainly a smart guy, and she loved his large masculine frame. He was much more appealing than most of the people she had to deal with.

"Come on then," she went on. "What's your voice telling you now?" She expected him to say something about her or the casino.

"It's wondering about all the possible worlds that my baby might have been born into. It wants to know why this particular world could not be better, why does there have to be death and meanness. It is sorrowing that things cannot be better. It is wishing they were better."

Barton gazed at the woman, as if she had an answer, but soon he realised the impression his words had made upon her. He saw the dismay on her face. He broke off his gaze, finished his wine in a single gulp and turned to leave.

"Where are you going?" the woman asked, more out of curiosity than any desire for him to stay.

"The hospital," he replied.

FACIAL SECURITIES

It was the morning after. Katherine awoke painfully. Her eyes scanned the mottled concrete ceiling, bleary, unseeing. She was facing bankruptcy. Getting drunk had seemed the only option. Being 'Westernised' had its compensations.

She decided to wear green to match her face. Livid Lincoln Linden green. The colour of sweet pastoral freshness. The colour of money. The colour of her headache. Bottle green.

She wore one of her linen suits. She had several of different colours. The one she chose was lime green. It had a tight skirt to the knee, almost hidden by the long flared jacket. Her blouse had orange sailing boats with white triangular sails scudding across an angry sea. It did not go at all well. But this did not matter on this pea-coloured morning, as neither did she.

At the office, she read the business news. The columns of figures took her mind off the faint nausea. There was not much to do. Facial Securities was running itself into the ground. She still put on a brave front and 'put out more flags', but the truth was that, unless something happened soon, the company was doomed. People, it seemed, did not mind losing face any more.

She was the only partner left in the firm. Will had taken up pig farming in Indonesia. Rop the cop had become a magistrate back in his own country where he was inordinately proud of his service as a member of the police force. Only she remained to juggle embarrassment, fashion and fate and continue to maximise the profit from each. It had been her idea at the beginning. In a country where the worst imaginable disaster was a loss of face, why not open an insurance company where if some great embarrassment should befall you, then you could claim on your policy and get some compensation. It seemed like a good idea at the time. Twenty storeys below the office, the streets were hideous; crowded, clamouring, hammering. People picked their way among the debris with universal, studied unconcern, all of them desperate to fit in and not be a figure of shame. If only a few of them would come up and take out a policy, their future would be secure.

OCTAVIUS HAD CHOSEN Saturday morning deliberately; he was a calculating man. At 11 a.m. exactly, he entered the office of Facial Securities and inquired of the temporary secretary Fuchsia if Katherine would see him. Fuchsia saw him in. Katherine looked up to see a strong, formidable-looking man who must have been at least 130 kilograms. He carried his obese figure with grace, however. He had a powerful, handsome face with luxurious glossy hair. He was dressed immaculately in a splendid business suit that was cut to perfection and did much to hide his large proportions. Automatically, Katherine buttoned up her jacket. The little sailing boats were sure to sink beneath the luscious texture of the Armani.

"The matter I wish to speak about is delicate, personal and singularly important," Octavius began in English. His voice produced the conviction that he must have worked as an instructor for BBC announcers. It was a beautiful voice, like an opera singer's.

"Most of our business is as you describe," she answered in her best confidence-giving accent and imitating his style of speech perfectly. She liked speaking English.

"It concerns a proposal of marriage."

Oh, is that all, she thought.

This was the most usual of all loss-of-face policies. The pride of people in this respect during the good old days had been her greatest money earner. Katherine felt suddenly like a dentist must feel filling the thousandth molar of her career. It looked like boring bread and butter stuff. It was not the salvation she was looking for.

Octavius continued. "I need a top-of-the-line policy. If anything at all should go wrong and the marriage not proceed as planned, I require a compensation payment of twelve million Hong Kong dollars."

Katherine's eyes sparkled, but she had to explain the situation.

"That is not the way policies work …"

She went on to explain that any failures would have to be specifically spelled out in the policy and that a great deal of investigation would be necessary before she could agree to such a deal.

"Special conditions apply, of course" was a sentence she repeated at least half a dozen times. To her great dismay, Octavius stood up at the mention of these conditions and appeared to be about to leave.

Katherine felt financial ruin creeping up on her from every angle. She really was in no position not to take this lifeline.

"I'm sure something can be arranged," she said. "But you'll have to give me some details."

Octavius hovered, waiting to see where this would lead. Katherine showed no undue reaction.

"I have no objection to your checking out my position in the world," he said. "You'll find that I am a man of some means. I do suffer from extreme shyness; however, the thought of any embarrassment appals me, especially if it were to happen before my family."

Octavius resumed his seat.

"I have it in my mind to propose to the woman in question, Dora, next Tuesday at a funeral. She is a cousin of mine, a very distant cousin, and I have known her all my life."

"But a funeral is hardly the place, surely."

"It's the only time I'll be able to see her. You see, she despises me. There's no question of her going on a date with me. The funeral is my only chance. I'm going to propose in front of everyone, this is why I need your policy. Can you imagine the embarrassment if she knocks me back?"

Where did that phrase come from? Katherine wondered.

Octavius realised his expression was somewhat colloquial. "So to speak," he continued. "I mean turns me down."

"Of course," answered Katherine. The deal was getting more and more untenable.

"Why exactly does she despise you?"

"It was because of Barbie; the incident occurred when we were six. I'm afraid I pulled the head off her doll. It was a rare model, a first edition with golden hair and a black and white bathing suit. One sold recently for twenty-seven thousand dollars."

"How do you know?" asked Katherine.

"Because I bought it, I thought it might help. It's in my briefcase. Would you like to see?"

"No, that will not be necessary. Look, I think you might have the wrong idea about what we do here. If you are so likely to be turned down, the risk is far too great. Why should I insure you for twelve million dollars when you are almost guaranteed to make the claim?"

Octavius considered the question only briefly. He clearly had his answer ready. "Because I'm going to pay you thirteen million dollars for the premium. If the family think that I've made money from your insurance, far from losing face, I will go up in their estimation. You must be there at the funeral and feign displeasure. This will convince my family that I have made a profit."

"I see," answered Katherine, who, for the rest of her life, took pride in the fact that she was able to show no emotion at this surprising turn of events.

"Well, in that case," she said calmly, standing up and moving towards the door, "if you wait for a few minutes, I'll get Fuchsia to prepare the forms and work out the details."

Outside, Katherine explained the situation. Fuchsia was a very smart woman and of course the first thing she said was, "Scam, it has got to be a scam. If by some chance the proposal is accepted, we stand to walk away with thirteen million dollars. It's got to be a scam."

The two women googled Octavius on Fuchsia's computer. In less than a minute they discovered that he checked out. His family was one of the richest in Asia with interests in shipping, hotels and banking. Octavius himself, who looked quite dashing in the corporate picture, was no playboy son. He had overseen dozens of successful businesses but was something of a recluse.

By noon, the deal was done, and Octavius left the building with the policy safely stowed beside Barbie in the briefcase.

THE FOLLOWING day Octavius rang in order to set up what he described as a rehearsal. It was to be a dress rehearsal in the funeral parlour. Katherine arrived on the appointed day at the appointed time in her black dress. It was the most exclusive funeral home in the country. It had the feeling of a sombre stately home of the kind you might find in Europe somewhere. Perhaps Dracula would have been laid to rest in such a place.

Octavius was waiting, standing beside his Maserati. He too was dressed very sombrely.

"We are to bury my great-uncle on Tuesday. He was one

hundred and four. He collapsed while out jogging. It was a terrible shock to us all."

"Right," was all Katherine said.

Octavius continued as they entered the building. "The coffin will be over there and just after the ceremony, when it is to be taken out, just before Dora leaves to return to Cleveland, Ohio, I'll declare myself. It's my only chance."

"Right," said Katherine again. It seemed hopeless to point out that this was perhaps not the time or the place or the way in which to propose to someone.

"Yes," said Octavius in a manner that tried to convey confidence but which merely enhanced his air of insecurity. "Yes," he said again.

That was when it happened. At that precise moment, as he spoke that single word, Katherine realised she cared what happened to him, her heart tightened with concern. It took her completely by surprise. She had long regarded her heart as merely a pump, ever since she fell for her physics teacher when she was twelve. That was quite enough of that, she had said to her teenage self. That way lies drudgery, but Octavius now seemed to her brave in his innocence and such a sad figure, drifting through the universe. Why was it, she wondered to herself, that so often the richest people seem the most wretched?

"Look, Octavius," she began. "This is not even close to a proper way of living. Dora will be a stranger to you by now. You will just seem crazy to her. It's not just about embarrassment or losing face, it's just all wrong." She didn't add that from a simple social media search she had discovered that Dora had already formed an attachment with a successful property developer. Why Octavius had not made similar inquiries she could not imagine.

Octavius raised his chin with some defiance. He looked striking in the soft lighting of the funeral parlour with its purple curtains and expensively crafted furniture.

"I think it likely that I know my own business rather better than you do," he said, not unreasonably. "Dora and I have a special bond."

Katherine had done much reading about this man's life. Sent away to boarding school at the age of eight where he had been relentlessly bullied then harried by a demanding father into a punishing routine. Pushed into positions of high responsibility from an early age, he had never really been able to grow up and then there was his obsessive eating and his gross shyness, which his weight must have increased. It seemed to her a classic case of a cold, jealous father who had pretty much destroyed his son's chance of a decent life.

She wondered what kind of special bond Octavius could possibly hope to have with someone he had not spoken to since he was six, some twenty years ago.

"This is what I'm going to say," Octavius continued. He then pitched into the most excruciating speech that Katherine had heard in her life. All about breaking mornings and golden sunrises and bringing up little ones.

"I'm sorry," said Katherine, "please stop. At best Dora will run out of the building and at worst she will laugh at you."

Octavius looked at her. It was clear that he knew she was right. He still had his pride, however. "What do you care? You'll make money either way. Remember, you work for me."

"I do care," Katherine was amazed to hear herself say. "I do care. I don't want people to laugh at you."

There it was. All these years exploiting the loss of face, as though it was a commodity like any other, something vain to be made use of but now for the first time, Katherine felt face to face what a devastating thing it can be.

Octavius's eyes softened. He could see she really cared about him. Not his money or what she could make out of him but for him, for who he was. He was surprised by her concern and because he had suffered such a lack of affection for so many years, he found himself moved by it.

The silence between them lasted for what must have been a

full minute, and then Octavius did something that for him was an act of great courage. He raised his hand towards her. She did not smile but merely took his hand in hers.

Together they walked out of the chapel.

THE MORNING GLOW

Turangi, 1957

GRAHAM NEVER NEEDED AN ALARM CLOCK. On a fishing day he would wake exactly on time and in less than a minute delight would force its way past the fog of depression that always lurked during the moment of waking. It was just as well that there was no alarm bell; his wife, June, would never have put up with being woken at 4 a.m.

All his gear was ready: his basket, his waders, his rods. It was December so already the eastern sky glowed with morning. Birds had begun to rustle and sing. He closed the door gently although there was very little chance of waking the kids who would sleep as long as they were allowed.

The road shone silver in the morning glow. It was only a couple of hundred yards to the bridge. He would have to cross it before starting inland from the lake. The path was not that well defined in the darkness, but Graham knew it well. He carried a torch but did not need it. It was going to be a splendid, clear day. The sun's scarlet rays had begun to pick out a few patches of morning cumulus. The moon was already outshone in the purple sky to the north. He could hear the river's song; easily, he thought, the most beautiful sound in the universe. Conditions were perfect. Some people would fish just beyond the bridge, but Graham always went far deeper into the forest. Everyone said how dangerous it was to walk for so long in the darkness.

Suddenly a strange call began, and he stopped amazed. It was a high, single, rising tone, repeated many times. He knew what it was but had only heard it perhaps twice before and that was many years ago. A kiwi.

Graham didn't think during the walk. Normally he loved thought and had spent his life dealing with problems and working things out. Freedom from thought was difficult to achieve but there, walking beside the river with his senses filled with the grandness of a new morning and the thrill of being alone in the bush, there was nothing in his mind except life itself. The rhythm of his body fell easily in step with the contours of the time.

Soon it was time to select his spot. How this was done was a mystery. It was a question of the 'look' of the water's surface and the fall of the light upon it, plus obviously the level of the river. It had rained steadily over the previous week so there was a good flow; some places near the centre would be too deep. Graham came to the inside of a sweeping bend where the water seemed still. He knew at once this was the place.

The chill of the water soon found its way through his waders; Graham knew that he was going to do well. He hooked his fly and with a swirling action all his own, he made his first cast.

It was 10.30 when Graham walked back up his drive, his bag filled with trout, although he had kept only a few of those he had caught. Some days he threw them all back but there were several elderly people he knew that he kept supplied with fish whenever he could.

The kids were having their breakfast. He had seen Jack Logan's beat-up Austin and so was not surprised to see him at the breakfast table drinking coffee.

"How did you do?" Jack asked.

"Not too badly. You been out?"

"No, too busy."

"Oh, yes, I'd forgotten about the competition."

Graham had, of course, not forgotten about the main event of the summer when some two hundred fishermen would cast from the shore of the lake aiming for the £100 prize that was awarded for the heaviest single catch. He despised fishing from the lake shore and despised the competition even more.

"We need you, Graham. Porters are sending a man."

"Really?"

This was a genuine surprise. Porters were the largest, most professional sports fishing outfit in the world. They were based in the USA but ran tours to every corner of the globe. Their clients were mostly millionaires and their staff fishermen guides were the best money could buy. These men were the superstars of the fishing world.

"If the Porters men like the place, we'll have the whole world descending upon us. It'll be the end of this village and our rivers for the ordinary sportsman."

Graham knew that this was true, but his view was that the employment the tourists would bring far outweighed any disadvantages. Since losing his job as the manager of the local timber mill, he had tried to support his family as a fishing guide, but business was extremely slow. June brought in more cash with her job at the local dairy.

The Porters team would be a revelation to watch if their reputation was anything to go by. He assumed that they would come with a large team and practise continuously for weeks and keep all their research a secret. After Jack was gone, Graham found himself excited by the prospect of seeing how the top professionals operated.

In the event, he was wrong about their methods. Porters sent just one individual who arrived in a hire car with the minimum of equipment. He was middle-aged, not much younger than Graham. During the two weeks leading up to the competition no one saw him out fishing, although he did take walks along the coast.

The local team held a meeting to plan their strategy. Some people suggested that there was not a problem, that local knowledge and the sheer number of people they would have out on the course would be sufficient to beat the Porters man. Graham was not so sure.

"It's a question of class," he said to the assembled group of local anglers. "I don't know what he's up to but these blokes are hand-picked from around the world. We have to try to do the best we can, and I'm quite willing to tell you everything I know. I go back forty years on this lake, but the odds still have to be in his favour, it's just the way it is."

On the evening before the contest, Graham was in the Lazy Trout having a beer when in walked the Porters man. He came straight over to where Graham was sitting. He ran his eye along the beers on offer.

"Tell me, Graham," he said. "Which of these beers do you recommend?"

Graham tried not look shocked that this man knew his name.

"Nothing beats DB," he said glumly.

"Word has it that you're the man to beat," the American said softly.

"Shore fishing is a lottery. You know that," said Graham.

"Maybe it is."

The man ordered his beer and said nothing for some time. Graham couldn't resist asking him a question he had always wondered about Porters.

"Why do you people have to win before you recommend a place to your clients?"

"I've no idea. It goes back to old man Porter in the nineteen twenties. I suppose he felt it was like winning the right to fish, like taking by right of conquest."

"You'll destroy this place. Some days I can go out and be the only man on the river."

"Sounds great to me. There's nothing personal here. I'm only doing my job."

"But it's only a game, a pastime."

"Now, Graham, we both know that that is bullshit." He offered Graham his hand. "Good luck," he said and with that he walked out of the bar.

THE CONTEST LASTED from six in the morning till midday. The course ran for the half mile that separated the mouths of the two main trout-fishing rivers just north of the township. The time was not the best and the place was not the best. Graham knew that most contestants would finish empty-handed. It had been suggested that the local men should crowd out the Porters man and not allow him a fair go. Graham and several others had stopped this happening. If he won, which was quite likely, the Porters man would have to do it fair and square. The fishermen of the area were perhaps not the best in the world and they certainly didn't have the latest and most expensive equipment, but they would keep their honour and their dignity, win or lose.

The day was cool and windy; a steady drizzle began just before dawn. At six precisely the flags were raised, and the competition began. Graham and all the local men were the first to cast. They had every available rod in the water, but the choppy surface meant they couldn't really see what they were doing. The largest single catch was always a lottery, but on this day, it was even more so.

Just before seven a huge shout was heard along the beach; someone had landed a ten-pounder. It was a stranger up from

Wellington for the day. The local men were ambivalent about this. On the one hand it meant they were out of it, but on the other hand so was the Porters man. The proud Wellingtonian made his way into the weighing shed. During the next hour many people gave up; they had never caught a fish that size even on the best days after years of effort. Graham would have packed it in too, except that he hadn't seen the Porters man. This worried him. Where was he? No one had seen him on the course.

At nine o'clock the news came through that the Wellingtonian had been disqualified. His fish did weigh ten pounds. The problem was that it was not a Taupo fish. The local naturalist who acted as scrutiniser for the event had had his doubts from the beginning, and on close examination after gutting the fish he was able to confirm that the fish had been farmed elsewhere. The chap from Wellington was last seen heading south at a rate of knots. The game was on again.

At five past ten the man from Porters was at last spotted setting up in a place equidistant between the two rivers. There was hardly anyone in this place as it was near the rivers that everyone clustered. Graham and all the local experts were right out on the shallow mud flats where the river still showed brown against the grey of the lake. The locals were amazed at the positioning of the Porters man. The man's equipment was very advanced, clearly the best of everything. As he waded into the lake, quite a crowd gathered to see how he would fare. The water was shallow at this point, but he waded further and further in, and soon the water was up to his armpits. It seemed impossible that he could control his rod at such a depth in such choppy water. But cast he did. And what a cast. The line went whizzing out for what seemed like thirty seconds. And there on that very first cast there was a strike. For a moment he disappeared entirely under the water, but his rod remained steady although very bent. He had caught something big, very big. When after quite a walk in, he made it back to the beach, soaking wet from head to toe and shaking with the cold. In his strangely fashioned basket, the like of which no one on the lake had ever seen before, there lay a huge trout; it must have weighed at least ten pounds. It was still alive, and he deliberately waited until several people, including a competition judge, were close by before he despatched the beast with a sharp blow to the head.

Graham did very well that day, catching several trout of more than five pounds. He kept trying till the very last moment at twelve noon. He was exhausted. The Porters man, showered and changed, was waiting for him on the beach where he had been watching for the final hour.

Everyone on the shoreline had been told and retold about the amazing feat of the American. Graham shook the man's hand saying, "Well done, you're a champion."

Graham didn't go to the pub that evening. For the first time in his life he didn't feel like fishing the next day. He figured that the only way out of this mess was to travel away somewhere to some city and get a job.

At seven o'clock there was a knock at the door. It was the Porters man.

"I wondered if I could have word."

"Sure," answered Graham. "Come in."

June was doing some ironing in the kitchen, the kids were playing a board game on the floor.

Graham introduced their guest and then led him into the living room. June followed them in and cleared some books and her knitting from the sofa.

"I am sorry to disturb you like this but I have a proposal," said the American.

June looked to her husband, who said nothing, and so she asked, "Would you like some tea? I am afraid we don't have any coffee."

"Thanks, that would be fine."

Before she arrived back with her best tea service, the deal was done.

Graham was to be Porters' man on Lake Taupo. First he would train in Canada and then he was to return home and run the agency.

June could hardly get her breath when she learned the news, she had been so worried for so long.

Before the Porters man left, they arranged to meet the following morning at 4.30 on the bridge. As the man went out the door, Graham said, "You know, I still don't know your name."

"It's Porter, Ray Porter."

THE ROMANCER

Mountsorrel, Leicestershire, 1922

ENA SAT by her special place on the bank and stared through the shiny water of the brook to its bed. The large round pebbles beneath the shimmering shallow flow were her friends. They had been friends forever. She had names for them and thought of them as a family. There were happy and sad ones, kind ones and angry ones. She would play a whole afternoon with her family of stone relations.

This day was sunshine and shimmering like the brook, but the water was icy, and the slimy grass always stuck to your feet so Ena didn't touch the water. Even the grass was warm except for where she was sitting. All was still and hot, even the sky. She listened to the trickling high sound of the running water. It sounded too high, too quick. It was like life was running away from you faster than you could run; even at night, even at your fastest at night.

Today was 24 August 1922. Ena was now ten. It was her birthday. Like always on birthdays and Christmas and Bonfire Night, she tingled inside. She smiled at people, who didn't know why. It was the best of times.

The day wobbled. There came a rattling from the bridge. Ena could see a caravan through the trees and then another and another. She raced round to the bridge and over they came. Five caravans painted a million different colours. They were not gypsies; they were players, travelling players — actors.

Ena ran across the field as fast as she could, jumping the cow pats, holding her breath past the new ones. Back at the house, she loved that she got to be the one who told. Ena had three sisters; two were older. Even Father came out to see the caravans go past but he looked with ordinary eyes. Mother did not live there any more.

The travelling show pulled up onto the village green. Ena was scared of the caravans, which were as big as the sky. They rolled and toppled heavily as the horses pulled them up. They took great divots out of the green at the strain. As the last wagon trundled onto the grass, a box spilled off. The kids squealed and Ena ran to help pick up the stuff, but some bloke cleared her off. A great big man he was. Ena gave him some cheek; she always had a lot to say for herself. She stomped away quickly and proudly. As if she would steal any of their stuff!

The sisters ran up and asked what he had said. She made up a great long tale that was quite untrue. She was a romancer.

Ena received an orange and a threepence for her birthday. This was much more than she expected. But everyone knew that she was Father's favourite. They didn't mind. It was just the way things were. The daylight lingered as everyone talked to the show people. They began to erect a massive tent. The voices got louder as dusk fell. As always, Father set the table for supper at ten o'clock. It was not until then that they were allowed to eat the new bread. Then they would usually have a story or act a play. Later, in the girls' bedroom, the day was rustling and alive even when it was dark. Ena cuddled into Doris's back. She didn't sleep that night, or so she thought.

On the way from their house to the village green, a wall which began very tall became quite small as you moved up the hill. As you walked up, the green was gradually exposed to view.

Every day after school, Ena would go up and see the Holloways. They were the people who ran the show. During the six months since they had arrived, Ena became more and more involved with them. She had given up all her friends. She used to play on the common at sliding down the hill; on cardboard in summer and on sledges in the winter. They would wrap up stones and pretend to sell them in make-believe shops. But no more of this for Ena.

She was so cheeky and quick that she had soon insinuated herself into the company. She was to be an actress, she had decided.

One Saturday the play *East Lynne* was to be given for the last time. On the way up the hill to play Little Willie for the last time, Ena was sad to be losing the best part she had done.

'You must not cry tonight,' she told herself. 'There will be other parts. It is only the audience who are supposed to cry.'

It was very cold, and she ran up the hill to keep warm. They gave her a meal every night, which was much better than she ever got at home. Father always did his best, but he had no job and no money. The family had to live on what Beattie brought in making shoes. Father hated Friday nights when Beattie would hand over her wage packet. It was the only time he was ever angry.

As her eyes came level with the top of the wall, she could see the lights that ringed the marquee. The light bounced with each of her steps. She slithered on the ice-covered grass as she walked across the last part of the way.

Mr Holloway was very nice and called her 'Little E'. He played the husband in the play. Mrs Holloway was very spiky; she spent much of her time squealing and laughing at nothing.

Mrs Violet Holloway, as it said on the poster outside, played the wife, Little Willie's mother. Ena hated being kissed by her on stage. Her breath smelled of beer. Ena longed to wipe off the slobber but she couldn't as she was supposed to be dead. The Holloways had a son of their own, but he couldn't do the parts; he wasn't the type.

You could not tell you were on grass sometimes but the stage was very noisy. Mr Holloway sounded like a horse banging about. The first time that they had rehearsed, Ena had become frightened at the way the adults were so wrapped up in their parts. Their voices were quite different, and they would change inside. Now she had grown used to it, and she could also feel herself change as she became Little Willie.

In the last scene, Little Willie dies. The mother had run off with another man. She only sees Willie once and that is when she is disguised as a maid.

Ena laid back on the short and uncomfortable bed on the stage, preparing to die. The canvas roof flickered in the lamp light and the shadows made grotesque monsters that moved about the walls. She squeezed the tears out of her eyes. This wasn't hard, as everyone else in the theatre was crying. The flickering silence became unbearably loud as the child breathed its last breath, which Ena timed to perfection. This was when Violet Holloway comes in with the famous line, "Dead, dead and never called me mother."

After the show Mr Holloway called Ena into his van.

"What would you say if I asked you to come with us?"

They went back home to see Father. Ena went to bed as soon as she got there. Mr Holloway had to speak to Father alone. Ena was in a sleepy ecstasy. She had left them downstairs. She was going to be an actress. All romancers want to be actors. That's why they tell lies.

THE MORNING WAS WHITE. Ena knew that she wasn't going when she saw her father. Her throat seemed blocked, and she got hot and red inside. She screamed. She fought. Father slapped her face.

Out of the house and up the hill she ran. The pavement made it feel like she was running backwards. Again and again Ena slipped on the sparkling frost. It would be all right once she got to the field. She could go. They wanted her to go. It would be all right, it would be all right.

The wall was wet because the frost had melted. It was sparkly, dark green and red. As Ena's eyes came level with the top, she could see the trees on the other side of the green. The green was much bigger and had changed.

Ena ran to the middle of an empty field. Her breath was gone. She gasped in bitter loneliness. They had left her behind. She had missed them, lost them.

Ena stopped running. She had no idea where they'd gone.

The green was hardly marked. There was no way of knowing where the stage had stood. That world had melted away. Ena was a poor charity schoolgirl and the world was her village.

She wandered down to where the brook ran between the now frozen banks. The large round pebbles were still there on the bed of the stream. They had nothing to do with her. They were just a pile of smooth stones beneath the frozen water.

THE ORMSBY TRANSLATION

Robert was almost crying with rage. He nearly howled out in frustration. "Witty," he whispered angrily to himself. "How dare he replace droll with witty."

It was a Saturday and, as always, at ten in the morning Robert had set out to the library in town. He would walk both there and back, despite the load of books he carried each way. He was a tall, slim man with wispy white hair that was combed tidily over his head with the schoolboy parting he had worn since childhood. His clothes were shabby but clean: a tired grey jacket and thick corduroy trousers, a white shirt with a blue tie that was too long with the knot tied too small. These were his best clothes, his Saturday morning attire. He had a dread of looking like a tramp and even worse smelling like one. It was true that he lived in a shed at the bottom of their garden, but he was always careful to wash thoroughly every day in the bathroom in the ancient villa that Duleepa and Kosala rented. He would wait until they had gone to work and then slip in through their back door. He was always careful to make no mess and to tidy the kitchen for them. They had been so kind to him since Mr Perkins had died. Mr Perkins' son, who had inherited the place and lived in Thailand, would have thrown him out for sure had he known of Robert's presence, but the young couple from Sri Lanka, who were both qualified doctors, had been unfailingly kind to him.

He was not that old, only barely fifty, and in good health, but what had been done to *Don Quixote* very nearly caused him to faint. He had opened the great Spanish classic out of interest, just to get an idea of the quality of the translation. The dreadful man from a university in South Carolina had even dedicated his new translation to his family. But it wasn't a translation at all, it was merely a ruination of Ormsby's peerless masterpiece. How dare he, Robert stormed to himself, how dare he. That morning in the library he took the book and hid it among tomes on computer programming. "No less than it deserves," Robert reasoned just under his breath. Robert loathed computers and indeed all electronic devices. There was no electricity in his shed.

The morning was destroyed. Oh, he would get his invariably disappointing modern novels and one or two of his beloved biographies, and he would still meet his sister Catherine for lunch, but his nerves would not calm down for a very long time. What an outrage. How dare the man. How dare he.

He gazed about the library to calm himself. How he loved this place. At least this still existed. Free for all to use. There was only this central library that was reliable, it was true. Those in the suburbs had hardly any real books, but here everything was still as it should be. That is with a place for scholars on the third floor, a wide collection of serious non-fiction, staff who smiled at you and seemed to understand the importance of reading to one's life. There was even a concert every Thursday lunch time. Robert had not missed one of those in twenty years.

The young man at the checkout had long green hair. On the whole Robert approved of his appearance. He thought it valiant. The man hardly noticed him, but Robert addressed the fellow in complete sentences as always.

"Thank you for your help," he said in a voice that he hoped conveyed sincerity.

Now that the supermarket had automated checkouts, sometimes this encounter was Robert's only human interaction of the week. Not that he minded this. People were a challenge to Robert. Whenever he was in company, he felt their presence a chore; it made him feel as though he were on duty. He had been steeling himself for his meeting with Catherine for days.

He walked out onto the street where the ruffians with skateboards performed their menacing tricks. They behaved as though no one else in the world existed. There seemed to have been some tacit agreement that the entire planet was their domain and that it was incumbent upon the rest of the world's population to keep clear.

He walked briskly past them, despite the heavy bag full of books, towards the café in High Street with his long confident stride. Despite his straitened circumstances he was not without pride. Indeed, on good days he could think himself quite heroic.

Catherine was exactly on time. She was the clever one in the family. A lawyer of some standing. She had, what the Americans call in their admirable shorthand, 'a life'. To Robert's dismay she had with her a gangly, blond young man who Robert knew could only be her son Douglas. Now there were two people that Robert had to perform for. It had been some time since he had seen his sister and many years since he had met her family. They lived in Asia, where he assumed they earned pots of cash.

Catherine greeted Robert fondly with love in her eyes. This surprised him and made him feel inadequate. He had no idea that she cared for him and it excited feelings somewhere beneath his sternum that he did not recognise.

"How are you?"

"About the same," he answered, shaking the young man's hand. "Douglas, I would have known you anywhere. Eighteen is a fabulous age to be. I envy you."

He sat opposite from them and instantly he could see trouble in their eyes. Something was wrong for sure.

"Still the voracious reader, I see." Catherine gestured towards his bag of books.

"Of course."

"What are you reading?"

After asking this question Catherine smiled and turned to Douglas. "This is a question that you should ask your uncle only when you have time to spare. He never reads anything without it filling him with ideas."

She was being nice to him. Robert hardly recognised her manner. Something had definitely changed.

"I am not reading anything of note. The last book I enjoyed was by Flann O'Brien. He was a disciple of Joyce. This is strange because I do not care for Joyce, but I find that O'Brien is fresh, poetic and surprising."

"See," laughed Catherine. "And that was just for starters."

"I was upset this morning," continued Robert, unable to restrain himself. "Some American fellow has produced a version of *Don Quixote* with watered-down English. He has mutilated the Ormsby translation."

"How awful," responded Catherine, seeming to mean it.

"There is one passage where instead of describing some action of Sancho's as droll, he has used the word witty. I mean really."

"But their meaning is totally different," said Catherine.

"I know," Robert said. "I know."

"Is *Don Quixote* a special favourite?" Douglas unexpectedly chimed in.

This was shocking to Robert, who had always assumed that he was the last ever teenager to devour the classics.

"Have you read it?" he asked his nephew. The answer would determine how he would reply.

"Of course," said Douglas.

"He's read everything. I can't imagine who he takes after."

How wonderful it must be, thought Robert, *to have a mother who is proud of you.*

"It is not a question of favourites," answered Robert. "It is that Cervantes did better what everyone else has been trying to do for the last four hundred years. He gave us a picture of the human body, mind and spirit as no one else has ever done; all of humanity is there. No one else has such range, not Tolstoy, not Proust, no one."

"There are long, boring passages. It can be really tedious." Catherine, who was three years younger than Robert, was a searching critic of everything; her views were always challenging.

"That is to do with the times," answered Robert. "The pace of everything must have been slower then. There are laboured and very dull passages in Shakespeare. The two men were close contemporaries."

"They died on the same day, you know. That cannot be a coincidence," said Douglas.

He found it quite comical how his mother and uncle answered together, their family connection unmistakable.

"What is it then?" they asked.

"I don't know, but it is truly weird."

There followed a pause. There was something big hanging in the air — a sad elephant sitting at the table waiting to be introduced. Robert wanted to help but how could he introduce the subject when he had no idea what it was.

"Are you still living in Mr Perkins' garden shed?" Catherine was delaying further.

"That is not really fair, it is hardly a shed, it's lined and quite spacious. It suits me very well. You know I am no good at working."

Robert addressed his next remarks to Douglas, even though he was pretty sure that the boy already knew his story.

"I have anxiety problems. Things get on top of me. Whenever I have had a job I start to worry and eventually I break down. I take Ritalin. I suppose you've heard of it. I believe some students take it by the handful."

"I'm not judging you," Catherine continued as though he

had not spoken. "The way you looked after Morris Perkins after Mother died was beautiful. He was no relation to us, after all. If fact, he was always awkward and difficult even when she was still alive and living with him. I don't know how you put up with it."

"Oh, there is no mystery there. Mother loved him, and she told me to make sure he was all right."

Another pause. Being jetlagged, they ordered breakfast and Robert felt he had to join in so he ordered scrambled eggs. Before the food arrived, Catherine decided it was time for her news.

"Jonathan has allowed himself to become a cliché. He has asked me for a divorce in order to marry a twenty-three-year-old."

Robert was never made anxious by a real crisis, in fact he was quite good in one.

"That's sad news," he answered. "What will you do? Can I help?" He knew as he said it that the question was absurd. What use was he to anyone? But he knew it was the right thing to say.

"We're coming back home. I'm buying a house and I want you to come and live with us." Catherine was using her lawyer manner. She knew from long experience that big things must be said clearly and without unnecessary trimmings. Robert tried to gather himself. As always, he knew he would say what was right for them to hear rather than what he really felt. Catherine continued.

"You must see that your present living arrangements are not satisfactory and are not viable in the long term."

Robert was perfectly calm. Douglas wondered how someone with anxiety issues could receive such news with such equanimity.

"Well," Robert said eventually, "if you are sure. I will try to be no bother."

There really was no alternative. They would never understand how happy he had been and what a chore he found living a communal life.

"Good," said Catherine nodding her head in a final manner. She knew precisely what he was thinking, but she was sure of her arrangements. She had already secured a job. This was for the best.

After they had left him to walk home with his books, Catherine asked Douglas, "Well, what do you think?"

"I liked him," he answered. "I like his passion, even when he is wrong."

"What do you mean?"

"Well, what's the harm of making *Don Quixote* more accessible to the modern reader? All translations are eventually superseded, and you really cannot compare Cervantes to Proust."

"My God," laughed Christine, "you are so like him."

Douglas did not speak again. A little later Christine remarked, "I used to be so frustrated by him. Only now do I see how valuable he is."

THAT NIGHT ROBERT lay awake for hours. The day had been so upsetting. In his head he composed at least ten letters of complaint to the professor in South Carolina. Never once did he consider what Christine had told him.

He eventually stayed lying on his back. This was a position in which he had never been able to sleep; all hope of rest was in vain.

"How dare he," Robert whispered into the darkness. "How dare he."

GABRIELLE

I saw Gabrielle as soon as I had paid my fare and turned into the bus towards the other passengers. It was twenty years, but we recognised each other instantly. She was always quick-witted. I could see that she had decided to give me the chance to ignore her. I, being slow-witted, did not. I smiled insincerely.

She beckoned me to sit beside her; she loved to talk. She was dishevelled and simply a mess. Everything was a wreck: the famous jet-black hair now unkempt and grey; the terrific figure, shrunken and stick-like. My mother had written that ageing had ruined Gabrielle; she simply could not take it. She had taken to drink; even suicide had been mentioned, I think, but I'm not sure. The only thing that had remained the same was the glow of her dark eyes, which even now shone in the old way.

How they had gossiped in the old days, the days of her prime.

"Let's face it," my mother had lamented, "she's the sort of woman men like."

She certainly was. She was a real celebrity. Her husband, Tony, had been a huge man, built like a wall. The lover, Noel, was a dark Latin type. What a time they had, the three of them. Noel would park his car in various places and try creative ways of getting to her door. He once got stuck halfway over a garden fence. He was always observed by the neighbours. It had been like a French farce. No doubt there had been others. She had been so full of life. How she had changed.

"Leonie. I knew it was you. Never thought you would do as well as you did. Sorry about your mother."

She still spoke in that deafening manner. She wanted the whole bus to hear; she wanted to entertain.

"It was quick though, wasn't it? Both with her and your father. That's something to be thankful for, isn't it? What have you come back for?"

As a teenager I would have been mortified to have found myself interrogated in public by this 'News of the World'. Now I didn't care any more; may as well get it over with.

"I've come back to live. My marriage didn't work out."

"Didn't you like it in Australia?"

"I liked it too much."

It was typical of Gabrielle that she didn't require an explanation in order to understand this remark.

"If you've been happy somewhere, it's best to leave it when things get bad. I understand."

She did too. She had never lived anywhere but two doors away from my mother, but she knew a lot about people. It comes from being a star, I'm sure. She'd been the heroine of so many real-life dramas. Nothing teaches like experience; at least, this is true for someone like Gabrielle. The whole town had benefited from the entertainment she had provided. But no one was grateful to her for it. To my surprise I found myself beginning to like her. She who, no doubt, was still universally despised by the community.

I considered my coming home as a kind of burial. The little country town had hardly changed except for the closure of the dairy factory. I was taking a masochistic pleasure in coming back with my tail between my legs. The place had moved on, and I was as alone there as I would have been anywhere else, but at least I had inherited a house to live in. I couldn't afford to buy one, that was for sure.

"I've been to the dentist!"

I didn't miss the magnitude of this announcement for I remembered how in the old days she had been mortally afraid of the dentist's chair. She would bear the most appalling toothache rather than make the trip. By now, all her teeth had yellowed, and several were quite black.

"I finally screwed up my courage. First time in thirty years. It wasn't too bad. He was a nice-looking fella; I'll wear my best shoes next time."

"When do you have to go again?"

"Next week. He's going to give me a complete refurbishment."

This was bravely said, but one could sense the struggle it would cost her. I didn't have to say very much for the rest of the journey. She continued in her loud, tactless manner just as she would have done in the old days. The only difference was that the suggestive pauses and coquettish little giggles were no longer seductive but merely pathetic. She had been so lovely, so desirable, and now it was all gone.

We got off at the same stop. Waiting at her gate were two figures: a huge man, built like a wall; and a smaller, darker, Latin type of man. They were both holding flowers.

EVENING SONG

1921

JUST TO THE south of the city of Leicester in the English Midlands there used to be an area known as Highfields. It covered several gently rising slopes that spread out from the city centre and had been built during the nineteenth century to house the people who came in from the villages to labour in the shoe factories and engineering works.

These Victorian structures had buried all the charm and distinction of the old medieval town under a mass of continuous slate roofs. The most impressive building in the area was the workhouse. It contained the insane and the destitute and many who were neither but just too old to look after themselves. Husbands and wives were separated upon entering the workhouse. This was a matter of expediency and was done without reference to the time they may have spent together.

For a stranger new to the district, the chief difficulty was keeping one's bearings in so uniform a mass of buildings. The huge factories and warehouses with their tiny disproportionate entrances were of no use as landmarks, for each resembled the other. Even the chapels and the churches blended in similar greys and black.

For those bred in Highfields, finding the way was easy. Every house was infinitely different from its neighbours if only one knew the place. Each home had a spirit, even a personality, created by all that had happened there. Old residents would know number 53 Clipstone Street, for example, as Mr Hemsley's house; him who was so hard on his kids and was so strict with his wife that she left him, and nobody blamed her either.

Before him, old mother Black lived there: her whose husband kept pigeons and died of typhoid, even though you could have eaten your dinner out of her drains. Before her, there was Wingy Armstrong who had only one arm and kept an illegal book during the war and could do amazing sums in his head. For anyone who knew Clipstone Street, the Hemsleys' house was full of character, quite distinct from next door, number 51. This was a lucky house; Mr and Mrs Grant lived there.

HARRY GRANT CAME out into the dying light of the cold November evening. He noticed the streets were wet. He tried to concentrate on his walking so as to be sure not to skid, for there could be ice about, and now he was getting on a bit (he was eighty-four), he had to be careful not to slip up. He had taken to falling over lately. He hated the humiliation of tumbling to the ground more than he feared physical harm. He had always been so proud of his strength, but now even walking worried him. He did his best to appear confident, however, pulling his shoulders back before starting his walk down to the pub. This was his one outing of the day. There was not a soul in the street, but his time with the Tigers (the Royal Leicestershire Regiment) had taught him to walk proudly no matter what and the habit never left him.

He set himself into the slope which a young person would never have noticed and put his scarf over his mouth. He looked in at the Hemsleys' front window. The room had no fire and the two children were bent over their books with one candle between them.

It's a dreadful shame how that man treats those kids, Harry thought to himself. *If I were a bit younger I'd see 'im off, don't you worry. The man's potty wi'is religion and 'is Bible study. It's a bugger how your spirit don't stay with you. That's the worst bit about getting old. You're thinking on summat and suddenly your mind's a blank and you don't know where you are. That's the awful part about it. I never think about God much, but I know old Hemsley's wrong to carry on as he does. He is an arrogant bugger, that's what he is. If God does exist, he wouldn't want those kids treated like that, not that I think he does really. It's all those buggers like Hemsley. They think themselves so important that there's a special God and a special world just for people like him. As though all creation were for his benefit, potty bugger. Horses are stronger than people, more beautiful, more noble. They don't go around as if the world were for their benefit, and they wouldn't be cruel to their foals either.*

Harry loved horses. Having worked as a carter for most of his life, he thought of horses' behaviour as proper and the standard for other beings.

He felt a bit tired when he finally made it to the Stirrup Cup. In his heart he was beginning to be afraid of this walk, but he would never tell Bertha.

The Stirrup Cup was housed in a building slightly larger than its neighbours. It was the only pub close by and its clientele was drawn exclusively from the surrounding streets. The publican was Bill Edwards. He was a quiet, thoughtful man, not at all the way one would expect a publican to be. He was a newcomer to the street, having lived there for only ten years. Harry liked him even though he talked funny, coming as he did from Derbyshire.

"It's a reet cald neet then, Harry," called Bill as Harry shuffled up to the bar.

"'Tis an'all, and do you know that bugger Hemsley's got 'em kids reading in the front room wi' no fire or aught ta keep 'em warm."

"It's a bad do," said Bill as he pulled Harry's jug of nut-brown ale, the same porcelain container he had filled each evening since coming to Leicester.

The bar was empty except for Bub in the corner. She was a widow of about sixty-five, always full of energy, usually busily helping those who needed it but very bossy and a terrible gossip.

"All right, Harry?" she shouted across the room. "Reg Hemsley ought to be shot. No wonder 'is wife left 'im. Mind you, she should never have left those kids."

"She wanted to tek 'em, but 'e wun't let her," explained Harry.

Bub already knew this, but she still thought it wrong for the mother to leave her children.

"Anyway, 'ow would she keep 'em?" Bill Edwards put in reasonably.

"She could have found some way," continued Bub.

"Anyway, the poor little buggers are starved to death as it is, and he keeps 'em away from school, you know. It can't go on, the board man will be round, you mark my words."

Just then Ron Sculthorpe burst into the room. He was a big, awkward fellow with a red face and a huge stomach. He worked for one of the new haulage firms, which had a fleet of motor trucks and no horse-drawn vehicles. Harry didn't like Ron, just as he had not liked his father. They were both stupid and crude. Ron was especially displeasing, as he reminded Harry of the loss of his last two horses.

It had been the worst day of Harry's life. No one would buy them. Fine carthorses though they were, they could not compete with the new trucks. Finally, Harry had taken them to the local common and just let them loose. It had almost broken his heart.

And now this Sculthorpe fellow thought he knew it all, driving all the way to London in a single night. He didn't know what real carting was. Harry moved to the pub door. He couldn't bear the company of Sculthorpe.

Just as Harry was leaving, holding his jug of beer carefully with both hands, Sculthorpe called out, "You crossed the street at a different place tonight, Harry. You always cross down by our house but tonight you were almost level with the pub afore you come across. Knew where you were going, did you?"

Harry made no answer as, a little unsteadily, he made his way through the swing door.

"You'll show some respect to Harry if you want to use my pub," said Bill Edwards after the old man had left. "He's still twice the man you'll ever be."

"Three times more like," said Bub.

Ron grinned stupidly.

Number 51 Clipstone Street, like all its neighbours, shone with cleanliness. As Bub often remarked, you might be poor, but you don't have to be dirty. Apart from getting meals for himself and Bertha, cleaning was Harry's full-time occupation. The house was always sombre and dark for the windows were so tiny, and the gas lighting very dim, but the woodwork glowed with polish and except for the damp patches the place was as good as new. They had not much to show for their sixty-five years together, even though they had both worked hard and there had been no children to keep. All they had earned had gone on living. The front room opened straight onto the street, and contained the best furniture and ornaments. It was dominated by a large round table, placed in the centre of which was a china bowl painted in patriotic colours commemorating the coronation of King Edward. On the mantelpiece were the portraits of Bertha's relations but they were all dead. Out of twelve children only Bertha remained and not one of them produced any kids of their own. Harry had lost touch with his family long ago. He had no idea what had happened to them. Harry never bothered lighting the gas in the front room as he came in. He snapped the evening paper out of the letter box and carefully made his way past the bottom of the stairs into the back room where Bertha lay. He started the gas light burning, which always took some time and didn't provide much illumination, but he persisted until it was going. The room was heated by the black coal range upon which the stew was warming. When Harry poked the fire, Bertha woke up.

"Did you meet anybody out?" she asked.

"Only Bub. She was in early tonight. We talked about 'im next door; 'e's got 'em kids reading in the front room, wi' no fire or aught to keep 'em warm."

Bertha was upset by this, but she didn't show it for she knew that to talk of it would only make Harry worry all the more. She had been a machinist all her life until her eyes got too bad and she became stiff with arthritis. She was quite blind and bedridden now and totally dependent upon her husband. It grieved her to think of how the kids next door were treated. It seemed so unfair. She had longed for children all her life and had not been able to have them. They had been such a handsome couple in their youth. Harry had a large physique and all the shifting of coal and furniture had kept him fit. She had been slim with long black hair to her waist, the prettiest girl in town, everyone had said so. But there had been no children, something to do with lead poisoning when Harry was a child. They had always been a sober pair, rather strait-laced, most people said. They never really fitted in with the Clipstone Street crowd, but they had always been respected.

Dinner was pigs' trotters, boiled up with potatoes and onions. Bertha hardly ate at all nowadays. Harry would get annoyed with her but what appetite could she have lying in bed all day?

After dinner, Harry sat Bertha on the bucket and when he had got her back to bed again, he got out the candle and the magnifying glass so that he could read the paper out loud to her. This was the main entertainment of this and every other of their evenings.

Harry began on page one and simply read every word until he reached the end. Often they would stop to discuss some article or advertisement, but nothing would be left out. Harry's voice would hum away in his best 'reading out loud' voice, and every now and again he would stop for a sip of his stout.

After reading, Harry went out into the backyard for a look at the sky, and to fill the bucket full of coal. This was very hard for him, and he was quite some time doing it and had to take several rests but finally he banked up the fire, got undressed and slipped as carefully as he could in beside Bertha. She was already blessedly asleep. She would go several nights without sleeping, but eventually she would have a good night.

One of the children child next door, Doris Hemsley, could be heard quite clearly through the wall sobbing. She had been sent to bed again with a hiding. It happened often that she would complain about her father's strict regimen only to have it inflicted on her even more strongly. Harry often spoke to her over the fence and passed her secret scraps of food. He could hardly bear to hear her cry.

Why should the innocent have to go through such suffering while buggers like Hemsley got off scot-free? He could not fathom it. If God is so good and all powerful and all the rest of it, why should he give kids to buggers such as Hemsley?

The man's not fit to lead a pit pony. I'd see 'im off if I were a bit younger, don't you worry.

With thoughts such as these, Harry fell to sleep.

In fact, Bertha was only feigning sleep. She knew if they talked, Harry would only get himself into a state about the child next door. She also knew that Harry had found it very difficult to get the coal in; she knew he was afraid of going down to the pub and how confused he was getting. Often he would forget where he was or what he was doing.

Doris Hemsley could still be heard weeping. It never occurred to Bertha that she might envy the little girl her tears. She and Harry were nothing special.

THE GREAT JO LEE

1936

THE YOUNG MAN appeared at my gate last Tuesday afternoon when I was pruning the roses. I couldn't imagine what he wanted, but then I saw his face. It was her face, round, clear and innocent.

"Mr Carpenter? Excuse me, I'm looking for Mr Carpenter," he said.

"I am he."

"I wanted to talk to you about my father, Jo Lee. I believe you knew him."

He was wearing a good-quality suit and his accent was very correct and educated. His manner was neither haughty nor deferential. It was the manner of Jo Lee, one of life's aristocrats.

THE BOY LOOKED SO MUCH like his mother it brought the memories surging back. I had met her off the boat all those years ago in Queenstown, which then was a sheep station and very little else.

With the help of Jo Lee, and by working with the gold diggers, I knew some Cantonese. I moved up and introduced myself to her.

"Carpenter, ngo hai ying gwock yan." (Carpenter, I am an Englishman.)

It must have sounded absurd because she put her hand up to her mouth and giggled.

She replied in English. "Mr Carpenter, Jo Lee wrote that you would meet me."

Even now, all these years later, the memory of that moment moves me beyond words. I was thirty years old and five years married. I believe that she at that time was around twenty. I felt like there was this infinitely precious and fragile apparition before me that would suddenly disappear if touched by even the merest puff of wind. Ridiculous, of course. She was strong; she had travelled for weeks to get to Hong Kong and then had done two months by sea to Dunedin and at that time it was five days more from Dunedin to Queenstown.

She had made this trip in the company of miners, some new and some returning. These were hard men, and it was almost supernatural how tough they were. Their attitude towards her was strange. They seemed to pretend that she did not exist, yet they must have helped her on the way, even though she was travelling first class while they were steerage. She had come through it all and seemed very grand in her heavy and fashionable Western attire.

Back then it was almost a day's travel from Queenstown to Arrowtown. She had slept on the boat as it came down the lake and as it was still early, we could set off immediately. I lifted her trunk onto my trap, and we were soon upon the last leg of her journey to meet the man who was to be her husband. Like everyone else she could not but be impressed by the huge mountains rising up to Coronet Peak.

"It is very beautiful I think," she said.

I was something of a missionary at that time although I was

far more useful to the miners as a doctor. That was when they could be persuaded to use my services instead of their own medicine.

I asked my charge how she was feeling, and she said she was "Very well, thank you". She spoke excellent English, which she'd learned from the missionaries in China. She spoke freely like a modern Englishwoman and must've had professional training from someone well versed in modern European manners. She was someone used to fine living and servants; she was in for a terrible shock. Jo Lee had told me her story. Her people had been ruined by the dissipation of her father who had gambled away a considerable fortune, which left her family suddenly destitute. Jo Lee had chosen very carefully. He wanted a substantial, educated woman who could help in his business. This is exactly what he achieved. He had paid her fare to New Zealand. Basically, he had ordered her up like one of the many commodities he imported for his shop.

I believe that even then, right from the start, she knew the effect she had on me and I felt certain that again, right from that first meeting, she felt something for me.

THE BOY WAS STILL THERE in front of me. I tried to pull myself back to the present time.

"Yes, I knew your father. Come along in, young man. I'm so glad to meet you." I shook his hand heartily. I felt like crying but hung on, desperately. There were tears in my eyes, and I hoped they wouldn't show.

I called inside to Dorothea. She looked him up and down steadily and then offered him tea, saying, "I'm afraid we have only Indian."

Naturally, after a few pleasantries, I took him down to the Chinese village. All I had to do was half close my eyes and I could imagine the place as it used to be. Full of purposeful men determined, hard and yet extremely civilised. There used to be smoke blowing about the place as they cooked over their open fires. We walked along the trail that led to Jo Lee's store. I pointed out to the young man the piles of stone that had been miners' shacks. There was very little left. The town was dying on its feet since the end of the gold. The miners' dwellings were all gone, except of course for Jo Lee's house. If you can call such a place a house. It was built from stone but was also incredibly tiny.

The bedroom was less than the size of a double bed. He had a vegetable garden on the slope in front of his door. He sold his produce widely among both the European and the Chinese community. At the time of his wife's arrival there would have been about one hundred men working the Arrow River. Everything they had was bought from Jo Lee. It was little enough because even at that time the gold was almost gone. No matter, these people in the heat of summer and in the dreadful winters worked like men possessed. Their meagre finds of gold were exchanged by Jo Lee. He saw to their transfers of money back home. All the men intended to travel home as rich men. They were stopped by law from becoming citizens of New Zealand. Jo Lee dealt with all their problems and disputes honestly and with great authority. It's surprising to me now how readily we all accepted his judgement. I was not the only European who often went to him for advice.

I took the young man through the settlement. Men had lived beneath bits of tin plate and under the branches of trees, every day waking up to intense, back-breaking work, hoping this would be the day that they would find their fortune. I tried to impress upon the boy (he was a boy to me although he must have been nearly forty) the power his father had over his community. He was their lifeline to survival, being the only one among them who spoke any English. The opportunities for corruption were everywhere, but Jo Lee was a good and noble man. He made a great deal more money than any of the miners, but he led them with honour and with wisdom. There was never any trouble in the settlement despite the frontier atmosphere in the European part of town. And this was due in no small part to Jo Lee.

The marriage took place at Chinese New Year, which was the one time the men stopped working. I don't know how he did it, but Jo Lee put on a wonderful celebration with all kinds of delicacies that I had never seen before. Some of the local thugs tried to intrude upon the affair; for a moment it seemed that things might turn nasty. Jo Lee stood in the way of white men at least twice his size and with a few short phrases stared them down and sent them about their business. Such was the natural authority of the man.

I could tell that even the hardest of the miners did not begrudge him any part of his good fortune. He was their hero. For my part I was jealous of him. Jealous to the core of my being for I loved his young bride. We cannot choose who we love, and I was sick with it. Everything she touched became sacred to me. Her presence was like a physical pain which I had no way of treating. My wife did not see it; she was full of moral indignation that a man well into his sixties should marry such a child. Dorothea is a good brave woman, but she has never been able to break out of the view of the world that was set out for her during her strict English childhood. She has always held herself apart, separate even from me.

There was nothing to be done. Two years passed, years for me of real misery and yet I could live through them for an eternity knowing there would be a possibility of seeing her or being with her even for a moment. My life since has continued. I have done some good, I think, but essentially it has been merely a blank.

One day Jo Lee appeared at my surgery.

"It doesn't work, we can't do it," he said, and I knew immediately what he meant.

"I suppose you've tried Chinese remedies?"

"I want a son, Carpenter. You help us, you see my wife?"

I tried to point out to him that as he was nearing seventy, the problem was much more likely to be with him. He would not discuss such a possibility.

"You see my wife," he repeated.

She came the next day and would not let me examine her. Instead she merely observed me with a strange defiance in her manner but I could also see longing in her eyes, of that I am certain. I stood before her for a long time in a kind of trance and then without any conscious will, I reached forward and cupped her cheek with the palm of my hand. She put her hand over mine.

She returned several times over the next months; inevitably she was soon pregnant. I was the one to tell Jo Lee. He was not at all angry, and I realised that he had managed the whole thing. It had all been one of his schemes. He knew what was going on. He had a wonderful capacity for reading what was in someone's heart.

"She is so young, Carpenter. It is face, neither of us can lose face. Who can say what the child will look like? She must go home."

I saw her to the ferry. She cupped my hand to her cheek again as she said goodbye. She was comforting me.

"You will write to me?"

"No, you have a wife, do not be such a child."

"But how will you survive?"

"He gave me money," she said. "I will be very well and so will you."

Jo Lee died in 1916 aged eighty-seven. He was my best and dearest friend to the end. By the time of his death there were no more Chinese in Arrowtown. His was the last grave to be dug in the Chinese cemetery, which was shamefully kept separate from the rest of the graveyard. It was beside his grave that I was finally able to ask the young man, my son, what had become of his mother.

"She lives in Hong Kong," he told me, following this up with, "Actually, she owns a shipping line."

"Does she ever talk of your father?"

"Never," he said, looking down at the ill-kept grave and the deserted, squalid settlement.

From the way he said it, I got the impression that he despised the very idea of Jo Lee. I forced him to meet my eye as I said, "You might think me an ignorant old man, but there is one thing I know to be true. Jo Lee, your father, was a great man."

SAND

1934

THE TWO MEN walked between the lines of vehicles down to Jimmy's bay. One was a customer, an airman in uniform. The other, Bill Norris, was a garage forecourt salesman. The lighting was poor and the concrete floor very badly stained with oil and swarf. Most of all, it was cold. The wooden walls were full of holes and provided very little shelter. It was winter and the large interior of the garage never had any heating except for the engines which coughed their fumes into the atmosphere. The man in uniform was about forty. He was below average height and sandy-haired. He had piercing blue eyes, but the rest of his face was without distinction. It was a long face, wide about the chin and out of proportion with the small body. It was the kind of face one saw everywhere in the north of England. Norris was a well-groomed man with an aristocratic air.

"Jimmy," said Norris, "you're famous! This gentleman has come all the way from Hull to see you."

Jimmy was even shorter than his visitor. He was a stocky fellow of about twenty-five years. He wore blue overalls that were thick with swarf. His hands were deeply engrained with grime and extremely hard and callused. He wore thick-rimmed spectacles and this made it seem that he had to concentrate very hard to see what he was looking at.

There was no formal introduction. Customers were not introduced to mechanics. Indeed, it was rare for customers to meet mechanics. Jimmy did not see it as his job; he found the appalling problems posed by the cars and trucks to be more than enough to occupy him.

Jimmy was a problem solver. The best around. He knew it and this gave him security. His manner was subservient to no one. Even in the Depression he would have been able to find work at any of the local garages. In his own way he was indeed famous. His manner was gruff and forbidding. His system was never to admit that any job was straightforward. This was the only wise course, for most jobs in practice were much more difficult than they first appeared. Just getting things to come apart was an art in itself once rust had eaten into joints.

It is the mechanic's lot to struggle and sweat over things an outsider might consider trivial and then to be treated as though his work is trivial. Jimmy was not bitter about this; he knew that he had won the respect of his peers and that was what counted. Customers, however, were another matter.

After Norris had left them, the soldier showed Jimmy his box full of parts. He spoke softly with no particular accent although Jimmy sensed he was putting on a manner he felt would be acceptable. This involved a slight mimicry of northern speech.

"It's this carburettor. It was in this state when I bought it at a sale. I'd like to fit it to my bike but for the life of me I cannot get it together."

Jimmy looked inside the box. The device had been stripped down to the last nut and washer.

"There was a chap in Hull who reckoned that if anyone local could fix it up, it would be you."

"Who was that then?" asked Jimmy.

"Harry Royle at Tates."

"Harry's a good man. Best man around on brakes."

"He speaks very highly of you."

"Are you sure it's all here?"

"No. Actually, I'm not, but the chap who sold it to me assured me it was."

"What's it off?"

"A Brough."

"Well, leave it with me and I'll see what I can do."

"I wondered if you could have a go now. Your manager, Mr Greensword, assured me that you would."

"Now? Why did he say that?"

The soldier didn't answer. Jimmy felt certain the man must have had some special hold on his manager. Greensword was a good man. Jimmy respected him. He would do nothing on Bill Norris's say-so, but Greensword was different.

"I'm supposed to get this back on the road for tomorrow," said Jimmy, indicating the heavy Bedford truck he had been underneath when the soldier had arrived.

"I don't think it'll take you long, if you know the tricks, as it were." The soldier's eyes were firm. Behind his well-bred diffidence, Jimmy could sense the strength of his will. He was determined to get the problem solved.

Jimmy took the box and carried it over to his engine bench. It was the only clean place in the whole building. He wiped his hands on a rag and began taking out the parts and carefully arranging them along the bench.

"Actually, I've made some drawings," began the soldier.

But Jimmy showed little interest in these. "They're no bleddy good," he said, his concentration already taken up with the parts. The soldier seemed somewhat crestfallen at this, but he got out his notebook and began making sketches as Jimmy progressed in his assembly work.

This was when the magic started. That is the only way to describe a gift like Jimmy's. It had gone back for as long as he could remember. He had never been able to write clearly or spell properly. His weak eyes had precluded much reading, and he was certainly no athlete with his short, stubby limbs. But what he could do, right from his earliest years, was understand machines. This was not from any scientific standpoint but from a kind of anthropomorphic sympathy. He put things together from an instinct of what felt right. He knew the basics of the science but what was far more important as far as he was concerned were the patterns and the symmetries — the configurations that he knew to be right, even when he had no rational basis for deciding that they were so.

At first, things progressed pretty much as the soldier had expected. Just as he had done, Jimmy arrived at a point where a cup-like enclosure had to be inserted within the moulded body of the carburettor. There was a sprung ring that he supposed was to have fitted in a slot, but he had not been able to get the ring in place despite hours of effort.

Jimmy reached for his hammer. The soldier knew it was impolite but he simply could not restrain himself.

"You're not going to hammer it, surely? The whole thing might smash."

"You got this far, did you?" asked Jimmy, not at all put out. "That's pretty good for an amateur, but what you must understand is that if it is used properly, the hammer is the most useful tool in any tool box."

With one deft tap, the ring was in place. The soldier had not enjoyed being described as an amateur, having worked as a mechanic in the Air Force for twelve years. He was also at least ten years Jimmy's senior. But the use of the hammer had been so skilled it brooked no argument.

"You're an airman, aren't you?"

"Until next year. They'll kick me out then."

"You'll get a tidy pension, I expect."

"Perhaps."

The man was obviously a gentleman, and Jimmy felt bad

about showing off with the hammer. The airman had an aura about him that Jimmy could sense was filled with experience and wisdom.

"There's not much to this," said Jimmy by way of playing down his work. "It's just practice. I dare say I wouldn't be much good on an aircraft engine."

"I work on boats actually. High-speed rescue craft. We hope to use them for getting men back who have pranged at sea."

"How fast can they go then?"

"About sixty knots."

Now, it was Jimmy's turn to feel like an amateur.

"They actually ride over the sea and skim across the surf. You can come and have a look, if you like."

It sounded like the invitation was genuine, but Jimmy knew he would never dare venture that far out of his own world.

Jimmy changed the subject. "I often take my bike out to Cleethorpes and ride on the sands. You should see the mess that makes of a carburettor. There's nothing worse than sand. It gets everywhere."

"I think I can imagine," said the airman with a smile.

"It's bleddy great out there when the tide goes out. You can ride for miles on the flat sand. It's like a desert. You can go flat out for as far as the eye can see. Sometimes, folks on horses have got caught by the tide but there's not much chance of that on a bike. I race speedway sometimes too. Never win, of course, ain't got the munny. But, you know, it's blokes like me that keep the sport going."

"I'd love to have a go at that, but I suppose I'm too long in the tooth."

"Get away with you. There're lots of blokes your age and even older."

As Jimmy continued to assemble the carburettor, he was quite oblivious to his unfortunate reference to the airman's age. The man could chat about the sands of Lincolnshire and fix together the complex assembly both at the same time.

There was one thing that worried the soldier, however. There on the bench lay a long spring. This belonged deep inside the assembly and Jimmy seemed to be leaving it out. Without the spring, the throttle would not be able to control the fuel flow. More and more of the parts were put together and still the spring lay there. The airman held out for as long as he could before saying, "I'm afraid that you've left out the throttle spring."

Jimmy just smiled and continued screwing in place the screws holding down the top cap.

Then, like the magician he was, he wound the spring around the throttle cable and into the tiny hole at the top of the carburettor. It went into place with a pleasing final click.

"That is amazing," said the airman. "Ten minutes flat. How many times have you made up one of these things before?"

"Never," said Jimmy.

"That's amazing," the airman repeated, and he put out his hand. Jimmy felt it impossible to shake hands, his hand being coated in swarf and grime. Instinctively, he moved to put his hand behind his back. The airman gripped the arm with his left hand and with surprising strength took Jimmy's hand in his and shook it firmly. They were silent for a moment and Jimmy felt he had to break the silence.

"It's a nice piece of work," he gestured towards the carburettor.

"Maybe, one day I could give you a go on my bike. It's the least I could do. Here, let me write down my name and address in camp. You could come and see me one weekend."

He picked up one of Jimmy's old work books and wrote out his details on the back. Jimmy knew he would never take him up on it, but he was glad to have been treated in such a friendly manner by a man who was obviously educated and well off. Jimmy read the address: A/C T.E. Shaw, 338171 RAF Bridlington.

"Well, I'll be going then. I'll be fitting it on the bike tomorrow. Come and have a go next weekend perhaps."

At this point Norris appeared.

"All right there, Mr Shaw?"

Shaw smiled at Jimmy, such a warm-hearted smile that Jimmy was a little embarrassed by it. It was a smile of one mechanic to another in the presence of a philistine.

Norris shepherded the airman out through the grimy path between the vehicles. He turned and waved once more to Jimmy from the entrance.

Jimmy felt a strange elation.

Norris was back almost immediately. "You know who that was, don't you? Lawrence of Arabia!"

Jimmy was preparing to get back under the Bedford he didn't reply but merely disappeared from view.

"What did you talk about?"

"Bikes and sand," said the voice from underneath the Bedford.

Norris quickly departed and so no one heard when Jimmy spoke again.

"He was a nice chap, but he knows bugger all about carburettors."

FOOTNOTES TO PLATO

It began with a dinner party that no one wanted. I met Gerry by chance. I hadn't seen him in years. He hadn't changed. It might have been the same ugly sports jacket he had worn throughout his university years. The black curly hair was still bushy with no sign of grey. The eyes, challenging and dreadfully sensitive, still worked behind his spectacles. His weedy frame had not filled out one bit. Most of all, he still had that disturbing manner that made him the least tactful person I have ever known.

"You've lost your hair! I almost didn't recognise you."

We swapped inanities, neither of us wanting to be the first to break off. For some reason, he wanted to keep up the pretence of close friendship. In fact, we had never been friends. I can't imagine Gerry ever acquiring a true friend.

We had roomed together in a student hostel. The first time away from home for both of us. We were put together because we hailed from the same town. He was the son of a GP, one of a long line of GPs. The scientific manner showed in everything he did, which was probably why he had started an arts course. I was from a long line of melancholic publicans.

I've often wondered why I've always felt so sorry for Gerry.

I'm not given to guilt normally. There was something about his clear scientific mind trying to grapple with the extremely unscientific business of living that touched my heart. He used to get so passionately upset about almost everything. There always seemed to be some attractive rival with a brain the size of a pea who would beat him to everything. For a long while, I was the nearest he had to an ally, and then Carol came along.

Carol is my wife. When we met, she was with Gerry. After Carol and I got together, Gerry disappeared for six months. When he reappeared, he had become a Christian and he had married. He had transferred to another college and had taken up medicine.

"What I find hard to understand is why you agreed to this dinner party."

Carol was not often angry, and she loved company, but she was not herself as we drove to Gerry's home that night.

"After all, you never liked him. He's sure to say something dreadful."

"You know how it is. When I said 'Let's get together sometime', I didn't mean it. He just leapt on the idea. I couldn't get out of it. He works at a maximum security prison. I suppose he needs to relax."

The house was very grand. It was at least a hundred years old and seemed to have been perfectly restored to its original condition.

"We did much of the work ourselves," said Gerry, standing in the hallway. "Some people from church gave us a hand." He was still gazing admiringly at his handiwork as he made one of his customary cutting remarks. "You're in one of those monstrosities down by the river?"

It had always been like this. Gerry would attack and the rest of us would try to make it all right. Yet, one felt sure that he was the one who suffered the most. I was shocked by the appearance of Gwen. She had aged alarmingly. She couldn't have been more than forty and yet she appeared wizened. I couldn't imagine what had eaten her up. There were three children, but Gerry's selfishness was the more likely culprit. Gwen was a most accomplished person. She made clothes; cooked like a dream; was a first grade tennis player and a successful sculptor. In company, however, Gerry would invariably take the lead. The one medium in which Gwen lacked mastery was words.

The house was clearly her work, but it was Gerry who showed us around. The kids were self-sufficient and smart in every sense.

"I hope you don't mind the children not eating with us. They're all working away on some project or another."

Both Carol and I were impressed by these children.

Carol couldn't resist asking. "Did you punish them when they were small?"

"Good Lord no!" answered Gerry. "One of the kids at school told our youngest, Jenny, that she had had a Big Smack. Jenny wanted to know if she could go to McDonald's and get one too!"

Gwen had prepared a great variety of dishes, all of which were superb and new to me. Gerry took her for granted as he had always done. She had never been pretty. When he first introduced her, all those years ago, it had been with a definite air of apology. One had always been able to sense that he didn't love her, but now his manner towards her had become bitterly cold. He spoke to her as one would to a family servant one had grown up with. It was maddening and pathetic. He was utterly dependent upon this woman who understood him completely and forgave him everything.

I was not expecting them to say grace and was very nearly caught out digging into the aubergine casserole. Gerry spoke to God as if He were sitting on the chandelier. It should have been embarrassing but Gwen's quiet eyes calmed the moment.

"What are you working on now?" I believe that Gwen had asked this question to avoid Gerry holding forth about himself, as he was sure to do before too long.

"I write software for the control of 3D images. Carol is the one who does the real work."

Gerry picked up on this and embarked upon one of his social atrocities.

"Still ripping off any poor sod who finds himself in trouble? I'd just hate your job."

"Would you?" answered Carol, who would rather die than show that Gerry had hurt her. "Someone has to sort out the mess. I'd imagine that what you do is hardly enjoyable."

Now we were for it.

"My job could not be more rewarding, in fact. I'm a lifeline to some of them. Much more than a quack. I am their lawyer, priest, social worker, friend — everything. Most are long stayers, twenty years and over, life in many cases. Murderers mostly."

He seemed to imagine that this lent glamour to his job.

"They are no worse off than any of us. They just have time to think about it. We're all in prison, don't you think?"

For some reason I found myself chanting Auden.

"In the prison of his days. Teach the free man how to praise."

Carol, who hated to hear poetry recited, said, "It's a very commonplace idea that goes back at least as far as Plato."

"It's still true," said Gerry, undeterred. "Life is suffering for everyone but working with the prisoners has taught me something which is not so widely acknowledged. We suffer because we hate ourselves. These men punish themselves far worse than anything the prison can do to them."

Foolishly, I rose to the bait. This was a shame, as it put me off the excellent food.

"But that is widely acknowledged. Socrates said as much. We should do the good deed because any benefit derived from a bad one will be far outweighed by the pain it gives our conscience. It's a cliché, the mental health industry runs on it. Religions have exploited it for centuries."

"Not in the way I mean. You see, many criminals indulge in

crime precisely because they lack what you and I think of as a conscience. What we all yearn for is forgiveness from something greater than ourselves. The cliché is that one cannot love unless one first loves oneself. Despite what the mental health people tell us, this is the wrong way around. Everyone can find peace if, and only if, we can truly recognise that Jesus forgives us. That is how we can escape from prison."

"But that is what all Christians believe."

"Of course! But in my job, I know it. I can feel it in the air."

The discussion was asinine. I could feel Carol's irritation with this man who seemed to be locked into an adolescent view of life. Poor Gwen tried to rescue the evening. She talked about her recipes and her art work. Gerry had become silent.

"What are 3D images?" asked Gwen, who also had the virtue of being able to listen.

"Holograms. It's amazing what can be done. I've got some in the car. I'll show you later if you like."

"What are they used for?"

"Advertising mostly and some scientific modelling and training work. Some artists have created terrific stuff."

I wanted to give something back to Gwen. It was juvenile of me, but I thought she might be interested in a new medium. Carol guessed what I was up to and for once did not pour scorn upon my glittering figures. I fetched in my boxes of tricks and wired them all together. We lowered the lights in their gracious hallway, which suddenly glowed with the image of a pop singer, followed by Nelson Mandela and then ravishing orchids and a section of a human body. Unfortunately, I'd forgotten that Jesus was also on the disk. He was suddenly standing before us. We had employed an Egyptian medical student. He did appear convincing. His eyes seemed to hold all the pain of the universe and yet his overall expression was one of infinite calm. Here was our all-forgiving Lord. He was going to be used in an anti-smoking ad but the sponsors thought the idea blasphemous. I turned it off.

"Well," said Gwen, "what is it that makes them so tacky?"

"They're dreadful, aren't they." Carol was so pleased that she had not been the one to say it first.

"I'm sorry," Gwen continued. "I'm sure it's very clever and everything, but they were quite dead. Quite without meaning."

In matters artistic, Gwen saw no place for politeness.

"Show me the last one again." Gerry's command brooked no argument. He looked positively demonic.

"Will they speak?" he asked, seemingly transfixed by the image.

"They can, but it's better if they don't. It destroys the effect."

"No," agreed Gerry, "it's better if He is quiet."

"Better for what?"

"You must let me use this figure at work."

"Don't be silly."

"These men are in for life. You cannot refuse to help them."

"I can't see what use these figures would be in a prison," said Carol.

Gwen didn't say anything. She began to tidy the dinner table.

I don't know why people did what Gerry asked of them. He had no charm whatsoever. He had the manner of a precocious, opinionated child. Perhaps I pitied him. If so, pity must be the most dangerous of all motives. Whatever it was, the following weekend, I found myself beside him, in his family four-wheel-drive, checking through security at the prison where he worked. We must have been breaking at least half a dozen laws. The men had not been informed of what was going to happen to them. No kind of permission had been obtained from the authorities. He had not even told the operatives in the hospital wing where the hoax was to take place. Carol was violently opposed to the enterprise. I don't know what Gwen thought. She had far too much good taste to criticise her partner socially. When we were setting up the observation channel in his office, I had to try one more time to dissuade him. I knew it was futile.

"One of the troubles with your theory is that you believe that these men accept that they have done wrong and are in need of forgiveness. I suspect most of them feel not the slightest guilt. How can you be sure that they all feel the same?"

"I work here. You do not. The weight of sin upon the heart is universal. Everyone shares in it."

"I don't believe in sin. My mind is not hung up upon the past. Look, you're a doctor. Surely, your responsibility ends with mending the body. You're a man of science, not a priest."

"We live by the spirit. We live in God. You speak the way you do because life has been good to you. You are healthy, intelligent and well off. You have never been tested. You are barely aware that you're alive."

What can you say to a speech like that? Several expletives came to mind, but they did not seem appropriate.

A private cell had been chosen which was next door to Gerry's office. It had been simple to wire through the wall and hide the laser transmitters. The whole time I was doing it, I felt the absurdity of the situation. I kept saying to myself, "I can't believe I'm doing this."

John Smithson was in for good. He was very close to death from complications associated with AIDS. He seemed to me a frightened animal. He lay in his cell, staring at the darkness. A wave of panic swept over me as the time came. Was it cruelty? Could I live with knowledge that I had tortured a dying man? I froze. I could have stopped the whole thing even then, but I didn't move. Gerry's faith never wavered. Jesus slowly emerged out of the darkness.

The most remarkable thing was that John showed not the slightest surprise. It was a magnificent vision. I had tuned it up to look perfectly real. A living God could not have looked more convincing. It glowed with beauty. It was the very essence of hope and forgiveness. John calmly regarded the image of God as living flesh for about two hours. He then fell asleep and died the next day without regaining consciousness.

Now, I was scared. This was way heavier than anything I had imagined.

"It was drugs. The poor guy was so far gone, he didn't know what he was looking at."

"He died knowing he was forgiven."

Gerry obviously felt vindicated.

"You're in too deep," he said. Any pretence of friendship had been abandoned. "You try to pull out now and we go down together."

I had no escape. In six months, we performed the hoax on about twenty inmates. Gerry became more and more daring. Quite healthy men were brought in after routine check-ups. Some of them tried to find the source of the light but none succeeded; the system is almost impossible to block. What is truly remarkable is that none of them talked. I suppose they were all afraid of being thought mad. Several of them were genuinely affected and wept and prayed at the feet of the image. Gerry assured me that these men found peace. As far as I know, they were never told what really happened. I was impressed by the bravery of some others who seemed not give a damn whether it was truly Our Lord or not. These people seemed in no need of any kind of redemption. They would just roll over and go to sleep.

My relationship with Carol was destroyed. She could not bear to look at me. There was something in what we were doing that she found utterly evil. I came home one morning to find my suitcase upon the front steps. She had always been the steady earner: the house and family were more hers than mine. I took a room in a boarding house.

I believe it was a staff nurse who informed upon us. We were caught red-handed one evening while setting up. My boss was one of the tough little party that burst in on us. So that was the end of my job. Our freedom from prosecution was made dependent upon our silence. We have never been punished in any way. Gerry was free to practise, and I believe he still does. The last I heard, he and his family were taking a cycling holiday in Israel. He refers to our time at the prison as 'The Experiment'. He seems quite unaffected by the whole thing.

I haven't been able to get John Smithson and the others out of my mind. It's made me quite ill. I'd like to tell you more about it but I must stop writing now. I don't want to be late for church. The evening service begins in a few minutes.

THE KEY

"Hello, Barbara, Roger here, how are you?"

"Fine."

"Look, I think we should meet again."

"Why?"

"Well, my key, you still have my key. What about the Green Room tonight, dinner?"

"No, not tonight."

"Lunch time then, Clouds. Twelve?"

"OK."

She never had said much even from the beginning when she first came to the yacht club with Lionel. They had all gone out on Roger's boat; she was very keen to learn how to sail, but she had hardly said a word all day. It wasn't that she was shy. She seemed confident with a mature and direct manner. During that first afternoon with a steady wind blowing and Lionel down below, she had presented Roger with a bottle of sun lotion and asked him to 'do' her back. Her look had been unmistakable. She had chosen him.

So they had their time together; they became what the people at the yacht club would call an item: each weekend on the boat, some dresses in Roger's wardrobe, a few bottles of herbs in his kitchen.

They had been together for a year when one afternoon they had a game of tennis. Barbara was quite expert and could meet Roger on equal terms. He ran down every shot and would hit the ball mightily but as his timing was so poor there was never much power in the stroke. Barbara positioned herself very efficiently and controlled the rallies easily. It was a hot, humid day and Barbara won point after point. It was too embarrassing to keep score, so they just played on and on, Roger serving correctly, changing court regularly and being his methodical self. Barbara was even more silent than usual. It was clear that Roger wanted to stop, but he was never one to take the initiative. He never said outright what he wanted from her. He would wait for Barbara to speak and fall in with her will. After an hour he was sunburnt and quite exhausted.

Finally, Roger made one of his elaborate serves into the net and they both moved to the centre of the court to retrieve the balls. She looked immaculate, hardly sweating. Roger was red and streaming. He bounced a ball over to her. He waited for her to speak; for a reprieve. She said nothing but steadily observed him and then she gracefully tossed the ball into the air and whacked it directly at him with all her might. It hit him heavily on the cheek. He rocked and held his hand to his mouth.

"What did you do that for?" he asked lamely, childlike.

"Because I wanted to see what you would do."

She calmly gathered her things and walked off the court. Roger ran shamefully after her, brushing his handkerchief over his mouth, which was bleeding slightly. They drove home without a word. Once there, Barbara packed while Roger kept asking what she was doing and whatever was the matter. After he had dropped her off outside her flat, she said "Sorry, Roger" in a manner neither angry nor completely insincere. They had not met since that day.

THE KEY

CLOUDS WAS a smart coffee shop in a hotel complex. It was very cleverly lit with blue and crimson shadows suggesting layers of cloud. It had a sleek efficiency, a little false in its American style of service but comfortable and welcoming for all that. The cuisine was very American with just the odd kiwifruit thrown in here and there to reassure the tourists that they were, after all, in a foreign land. Roger would never have lunched there normally. Being somewhat mean in small things, he usually visited fast food stalls. He had the ability to eat the same things each day for years at a time. He decided to have the buffet; it was such good value.

He was nervous. He hadn't seen Barbara for three weeks and she was late. He was a mechanical engineer by profession and was keenly interested in machines and had a very acute eye for detail. He would notice minute intricacies of designs and in his spare time would work happily for hours, on model aircraft or clocks with great patience and ingenuity. He would always see a project through to its completion. Perhaps that was why this business with Barbara was so upsetting, so damned strange. They had a reasonable time together. She enjoyed going out on his boat, *Rogercraft*. What had gone wrong?

He meant to find out over this lunch. Talk it through. Once and for all, get things sorted out. A heart to heart, he thought to himself. He would demand a reason. Sit her down and talk it through. Analyse the problem. Surely there could be nothing irrevocable and he not know of it.

Barbara arrived only two minutes late. Her presence stirred his heart more than he expected. He felt relieved to be with her again; it was a release from a steady ache he had grown not to notice until he felt its absence. He took in every detail of her appearance: the way her hair curled to her shoulders, luxuriant in coppers and golds; her freckles, her clear blue eyes, her skin incredibly fair and delicate; the knit of her jersey, the design of her tartan skirt with its golden safety pin about one third along its length. Her stockings and black low-heel shoes with golden triangular buckles. All this he saw and would remember, but he never thought to try to read her expression, to guess how she felt.

Barbara noticed very little of Roger's appearance. She felt only the pressure of his unconscious pleading. She considered this lunch a tiresome duty and as soon as she saw him, she realised it was a mistake. She was determined not to feel guilty but as Roger was so innocent, this was extremely difficult. He was a big man and was never afraid to behave in a courteous manner. He stood as she entered and smiled as warmly as he was able. He felt that as she was so attractive, such a welcome was her due. He always reasoned in this way, measure for measure.

"I'm glad you could come," he began. "The traffic was so bad, I had to walk here."

"Yes, it's awful at this time of day."

"It used to be that one o'clock was the busy time, but lunch seems to move earlier and earlier these days."

"Indeed."

She began to read the menu. He gazed at her, thinking she was unaware of it, but of course she felt his eyes examining her. He was always so open. Never had she known him to dissemble. She always knew what he was thinking and what he wanted from her. It was simple, unequivocal. It had been nice for a time but now it was embarrassing, impertinent. The waitress came over to take their order. Barbara chose the buffet, for she knew that this would please Roger. She had no desire to hurt him.

"Yes, I knew you'd choose that," said Roger, a smile lighting up his face.

She found this very irritating. Why should she feel she had to choose all those tables full of stodge? Roger had assumed that she would fall into his way of looking for the best deal, the most efficient order. It annoyed her.

Well, she seems all right, thought Roger. He noticed how

beautifully the colour of her hair went with the decor and that the cutlery laid before them had been manufactured in China.

Barbara felt like a witness at an inquiry, waiting to give evidence. Whatever was the point of this meeting? After all, didn't he know it was all over? Perhaps she should try to say something. But no, she considered, there was no use making points he would never understand. Why make him resentful? They went to the buffet table and Roger heaped food upon his plate; delicate fish and cold meat cuts with thick slices of roast beef and all manner of sauces. He went back twice for more and then had three desserts. He cleaned everything from his plate. He ate in a fixed order: green vegetables first, then starch vegetables and finally the meat, cutting things into perfectly square sections. He hardly spoke while eating, so intent was he on the process of taking in nourishment.

When the coffee had been served, Roger asked, "Was it raining when you came in?"

"Pouring."

"We've had such a hot spell, it's good to get some rain at last. The average temperature must be close to last year's."

"Yes, I remember it was warmer last year."

"Oh, yes, much. Last year was neat. We were able to get out on the boat every weekend." He felt happy talking to her again. He was beginning to feel sure that things were back to normal. He continued on about the weather, comparing it with other parts of the world and discussing the reliability of barometer readings.

Barbara considered him as he went on. She decided he was unaware of how he was trying to bully her into accepting that everything was as it had been, making a weapon of pity. He wasn't to blame but that didn't make it any more bearable. She interrupted him. "Well, I think I should get back now."

"But you don't start until two."

"I don't work there any more."

It was a break, something new in her life he didn't know

about. She looked directly into his eyes and waited for his next words. It was then that she felt completely released, for all she could see in him was fear. Roger was full of panic.

Later, he rehearsed the things he should have said at that moment. As it was, he simply didn't have the heart. Something in him flinched from a contact so vital. He raised his eyes over her shoulder and out of the window.

"It's stopped raining." He looked back at her and then away again, ashamed.

Barbara took her purse out of her handbag.

"Oh, I'll pay," said Roger grandly, but he was mistaken.

She was not looking for money. She was searching instead for his key. She placed it onto the table. She nodded her goodbye and was gone.

DIPA'S DEMON

"The trouble with my writing is that I'm not driven. What I need is a demon to kick me up the bum."

"Ah, like D.H. Lawrence."

Dennis was in Dipa's Dairy buying his tin of mushroom soup. Dipa was hearing once again of the would-be writer's trials and rejections. Dipa was wonderfully calm and being literary she knew all about demons and D.H. Lawrence's bum.

"You see, I get terrific ideas at all times of the day and night, but I just can't get them down, or at least when I do get them down, they come out all wrong. I need a demon to push me along."

Dennis's flow was interrupted by Archie, the Samoan guy.

"Dipa, I need some glue for me bike."

It was a miracle how she had everything that everyone asked for. She never had to look; she would sweep along the crowded shelves of the dimly lit shop and it would appear. It was uncanny: tropical fruit, exotic herbs, all manner of hardware and confectionery; it all found a place in Dipa's Dairy.

Dennis thought he was being funny when he said, "I don't suppose you could sell me a demon?"

Dipa smiled thoughtfully and slipped smoothly into the back room.

Well, he thought, *I suppose she could hardly keep them in her shop window.*

She glided back through the plastic string curtain, serene and as graceful as an Abyssinian cat. She held in her palm a tiny purple capsule the shape of a torpedo.

"I think this will do it," she said, dropping it into his hand. "Take it tonight before you sleep."

Dennis accepted the pill, but he was by no means sure. Freshly picked lemons from her back garden were one thing, a new distributer cap for his friend's ancient Triumph 2000 was even better, but not drugs. No, there was something not acceptable about drugs, even from Dipa.

"Any evil that follows from this will not come from this pill. It is quite harmless, believe me."

And he did believe her.

He had known her for five years. She and her mum and dad had taken the place over from old Bingly, who ordered biscuits one packet at a time. In his day the dairy was more often without milk than with it. The place had echoed with emptiness. Nowadays Dipa's parents stayed in the background smiling amiably, stocking and restocking the creaking shelves. Now everyone came and everyone was served. He had never seen her anywhere except behind the counter, always alert, patient, tranquil and indeed altogether immaculate. She had fixed opinions but argued with no one, quite a trick that. He had never known her to be wrong about anything.

"There's nothing in it that can hurt you. It's not LSD or anything. Do you want to write well or not?" She smiled and he suddenly felt a fool for doubting her.

He turned to walk out.

"That will be five dollars twenty-five cents."

He fumbled for the money he was saving for emergencies.

Dipa rang the till. There was very likely a button marked 'Demon Pills'.

After Dennis had gone, Dipa's father half emerged, the plastic beads strewn over his shoulder, looking greatly displeased.

"Oh, Father," she said. "You worry too much."

But she was not able to pacify him as easily as her ambitious customer — the would-be novelist who had just gone out into the night.

Dennis lived in a two-storey block of derelict flats that had the grand appellation 'Rialto Court'. He was on the first floor. They were built along an unadopted road that had fallen into disrepair and this matched the state of the apartments. The building was made from bare concrete blocks and was solid enough, but it was years since anyone cared about the upkeep of either interior or exterior. This bothered Dennis no end; artists of his type were not supposed to notice squalor, but he liked things tidy and was always having to fight off the desire to clean his place up.

It was dark as he turned into the unmarked track that led to his home. It took an act of faith to walk the fifty metres along the pot-holed, mud-filled track to his two-room home. It was utterly, totally, absurdly black. He stumbled along, fear fizzing about his collar, the purple pill still clutched in his fist. He scratched away with his key for the right lock. He had once tried to enter his next-door neighbour's door; the consequent encounter with the Rottweiler that lived at that address had not been pleasant. Feel and faith finally got him into his kitchen.

The dirty pots in the sink lured him for a moment but he held on to his principles and left them to moulder. The other room had posters of his heroes about the walls. The great men of letters stared down glumly at his bed and the table that served as his desk.

He had tried so very hard for so very long. He wanted to create something beautiful. He had attended perhaps twenty writers' workshops and dozens of summer schools. He had been a brutal realist, a Romantic Impressionist, a naive pop culturalist. All he had to show for it were two hundred and seventeen rejection slips. Still he kept on. There was the time a teacher at the local tech had advised him to travel, so he had travelled from Morrinsville to Montreal. It did not help. One published novelist at a summer school had suggested that he lacked experience of the underbelly of life; the despair of destitution. She herself drove a Merc, but never mind. Off he went with the glue sniffers under the motorway and the alkies on the park bench. It left him ill for months but still the rejections fell steadily through the letter box. No matter, still he kept on.

He put the purple demon pill onto a saucer beside the can of cold mushroom soup that was his meal for the day. The paraffin lamp provided light but not enough heat for cooking. His luxury was pepper; cold mushroom soup is not too bad with lashings of pepper. He had not applied for any state benefit. He felt that it would soften him, weaken his resolve. Would we have heard of Chekhov had the Tsar paid his debts for him? Dennis thought not.

Dennis had never taken drugs, even during his time with the people of the underbelly. He was in truth a bit of a puritan. This did seem like cheating. He was about to throw the capsule out into the blackness but then he remembered Dipa. A sense of her lovely compassionate presence swept over him. He threw his head back and swallowed hard. He blew out the lamp and felt his way onto the damp mattress which lay on the floor.

Suddenly it was light, bright white light that did not flow in through the window but seemed to emanate from every article of furniture. The room was clean, warm and above all peaceful. Outside, instead of the railway yard, there was native bush, primeval and rich and green as a jungle. Ferns and ponga trees towered above. The room nestled under the shadows of the waving trees.

At the table sat the demon. He was a very ordinary-looking silver-haired man. He wore a white linen suit with a white shirt and a bow tie. He was reading Dennis's latest production. He looked up when he saw that Dennis was alive to his presence.

"I won't laugh at you," he said in a soft cultured voice. "I can see that you have tried hard. There is some merit in this, not much, but some."

"Are you my demon?"

"Probably, I think of myself more as a toll collector, and the bearer of perilous news." He looked bored and not at all threatening. "I suppose you want to be famous, be a bestseller and all that."

"No," Dennis protested, "that is not it at all. I want to create something beautiful."

"Now why would you want to do that? Face it. You're just a vain little scribbler who wants to be loved. Why not admit it?"

"You're supposed to help me, not destroy my hopes."

"No, not at all. You said you wanted a demon to drive you on to good work. That is not help. Is a slave helped by his master? No, he is abused by him."

"I just want to create one beautiful book, to write one thing that is a true work of art. I don't even care if no one reads it."

The demon smiled at this. "You have no idea," he said. "None."

The two seemed to have reached a stalemate. There was a long pause. Finally, the demon appeared to have made a decision, though he still seemed bored by the whole business. It was as if he had seen everything that would happen a thousand times before.

"Here's the deal," he said as Dennis suddenly shivered in his warm four-poster with the starched linen sheets folded under his chin.

"Tonight you will write a story. It will be unlike anything you have done before. I mean it will be a very well written, truly beautiful work of art. Tomorrow when you wake you can read what you have done. You can then make your decision. If you show the work to any other living creature, you are mine and together we shall know greatness, by which, of course, I mean great suffering. In any event, for the rest of your long life you will write like a genius. If, on the other hand, you destroy the story by midday, from then on you are free to live as you please but you will never write well again.

"I advise the second option, but I have no doubt which one you will take."

It was as though someone had stopped a recording halfway through the word 'take'. Suddenly his chair was empty.

When Dennis woke, after eleven the next morning, all was as sordid as ever. The disappointment bit into his heart. It was a tedious dream, not even a fantastic dream, and yet the loss of it filled him with despair. How low he had come that even his dreams were stale and trite. He could have cried but he did not. What was the point? Even his unhappiness was dull and commonplace. He lifted himself out of his bed and turned to the table.

There it was! Seven pages of closely written script. Not a single word had been crossed out. It was in his hand, no doubt of that. He then noticed that the paraffin lamp was empty, yet he clearly remembered extinguishing it the night before. He sat and read. At the end he sat back in a state of pure shock and after a few minutes read again.

It was called 'The Age That You Are Now', and it was perfect. It was undoubtedly his. It was all drawn from his experience; every image and every nuance had been distilled from the thousands of scraps of paper he had filled over ten years of work. It was as good as anything he could have hoped for. How he loved the story. He had never known joy before. He had never even believed in its existence. What had life been until then? A symphony of disappointment and rejection in all the keys of the scale. There was nothing he could remember that could compare with this. No Romeo or Juliet in the ecstatic bliss of innocent first love could feel more. His body bubbled and trembled with happiness; he literally swooned with gladness.

It was half past eleven when he came round, and the demon's strange proposition came into his mind. What did the strange being mean? What were the options? What choice was there to be made? Obviously he would do his damnedest to share his story with all mankind. What did the demon mean when he referred to 'great suffering'?

This was when the puritan in him began whispering into his conscience. He felt certain nothing was bought without a fee, a toll, as the demon put it. He remembered the misery just about all the really first-rate artists have had to endure. But then Dennis realised that all this did not matter; he had known pure joy; he had made something beautiful. The demon did not really know him at all. He took the lighter he used for lighting his lamp and put the flame to the pages, but suddenly into his mind came all the people who would never know the joy of his story. What if Chekhov or Mansfield had burned their stories? How much would have been lost then? He put out the flame. It was eleven forty-five. He could think of only one person who would be able to help him make his decision. Dipa.

He grabbed the story and ran to Dipa'a store. She was busy. Two kids were choosing penny treats from the sweet jars with a slowness that Dennis found painful. Dipa wrapped up the little parcels of liquorice and sugar drops.

"I've got to talk to you."

Dipa's brow became less smooth as Dennis told his story. He kept saying "God! Look at the time", which as a religious woman she did not like at all.

"I don't understand," she said. "You're not making any sense at all."

"Don't you see?" said Dennis in desperation. "My whole life may be blighted."

It was too late, the clock in the library tower across the road began to strike and everyone knew that it was always at least five minutes slow.

"Dipa!" Dennis cried in despair. "What have you done?"

He could not bear that his fate had been taken out of his hands. He slumped down onto a pile of Sunday newspapers, his head in his hands.

"Here," said Dipa tenderly, "have one of these."

She offered him one of the jars that the two kids had been choosing from. The sweets inside were called 'Dolly Mixtures'. They were of many different shapes and sizes but one in particular caught Dennis's eye. It was a tiny purple capsule the shape of a torpedo.

NOT HIGH ENOUGH

"Without her money, she would be nothing."

"It's much worse than that. Even with her money, she is nothing."

She was just below them, they were on deck and she was in the bow of the yacht. A hatch was open. She wasn't meant to overhear them.

Bella sat down on a bunk and wondered what to do. The first speaker was her personal assistant, Maude, her servant really, and in some respects her paid companion. The second was her husband.

Maude was a French woman of impeccable qualifications. She spoke five languages and she dressed and spoke with immense taste and style. Bella had employed her after interviewing some twenty applicants. They had never been friends. After she had inherited her father's two hundred million, Bella quickly came to understand that she would never have any true friends. Bella had, however, been kind to Maude and had treated her as an equal. She had never given out orders or specified any particular duties. Maude was simply a companion. Bella had hoped to learn from her, she had hoped to acquire something of her confidence and poise. This had not happened. Instead Bella had found herself somewhat dominated by her assistant's arrogance. Strangers often mistook them. It was Maude who seemed to personify the very essence of a high-class heiress. Maude was more impressive in every way; she was taller, more beautiful and much more intelligent.

Bella's husband was Portuguese. They had met on a beach in Pernambuco. She had known from the start that this penniless man was on the make. He had never had a job as far as she knew although he was an excellent dancer and could perhaps have made a profession out of that. Bella had never been really good at anything, but she loved to dance. They danced together for hours and Bella had loved those times, but eventually she became aware that he was frustrated by her lack of talent. He still begged her to dance and occasionally they did, but they had stopped competing in the Latin festivals and didn't practise seriously any more.

Bella knew he had never loved her, but she had turned away from this fact continually. She forced herself to ignore it because she had so loved him. There was something in his look and in the way he moved that captivated her. He was five years younger than she was and Bella had seen in the eyes of everyone who knew them that they all understood the situation. His attempts to prove his ardour for her were pathetic. She had often considered asking him to stop, but she knew that for the sake of his pride he had to try to convince himself that his life was not that of a kept man, but clearly it was. He fooled no one.

Amazingly, it had never occurred to Bella that Maude and her husband would become confidants, let alone lovers. How dumb this seemed now. She thought that Maude despised him for his total lack of sophistication and the complete absence of manners and learning. She had often seen Maude wince when her husband spoke his mangled English with an accent that clearly irritated her.

As she sat on the bunk below them on the deck, she could hear that they were still speaking, but Bella made no more attempts to make out the words. She had heard enough. There was more communication and companionship in that single exchange than she had ever enjoyed with anyone. Their closeness was in the tone of their voice. Bella knew all there was to know.

The question still hung in the air. What should she do?

She could have ruined them and sent them ashore, penniless in this remote country. Bella knew at once that she would not do this, for the thing that hurt most was not the multiple betrayals. It was not jealousy or sexual passion. What hurt the most was the bringing to the surface what she knew to be true. What would she be without the life her father's money had made for her? Was she indeed nothing?

Dear God, am I?

What she did next was undertaken quickly and as if she was following some pre-ordained plan, and yet there was no thought involved. She got her swimming bag and bundled a few essential items and the money she had in her purse into it. She left behind her passport and credit cards and indeed every mark of her identity.

She slid from the back of the boat, which faced the shore, and swam to the beach. No one had seen her go. Before leaving she ordered the skipper to set sail back to the city about fifty miles across the wide bay.

Bella walked to the nearest village and from there she got a bus to the other side of the country. It was her first trip on a bus, and she found it horrible. She knew already how stupid and vain she had been. There was sure to be a search, with her picture in every paper and on television. There was no escape for someone in her position.

Bella supposed she would have to get a room in a motel until she was discovered. Having finally dismounted from the bus, being able to stand it no longer, she found herself in a tiny settlement that had no accommodation whatsoever. Her only option was at an orchard where gangs of migrant workers were picking apples. There was a shortage of labour and no one asked any questions. That evening she found herself watching the evening news with bronzed students from all over the world. She was the oldest there by at least ten years. There was nothing about her on the news.

The next day was appalling. The work was back-breaking and dreadfully dull. The food was equally bad and the money a pittance. She felt she couldn't stand another similar day. She realised once again how dumb she'd been. She knew that on discovery all that would happen would be that everyone would laugh at the poor little rich girl making a fool of herself again. She was wrong.

Nothing appeared in the press. There was no search. As the days passed, her hands became blistered, every muscle in her body ached and her skin was red and burned. No matter how bad it got she could not bring herself to go back. It was not pride, but a strange lassitude prevented her from acting. She moved from farm to farm with the gang. No one asked her any questions or bothered her at all. The young men who made a mission of pursuing every other woman in the gang completely ignored her. The women were pleasant but distant; they too seemed to barely notice her. Three months went by and the picking season came to an end. The workers were paid off in a small seaside town. When her fellow workers went back to their lives, they hugged each other and exchanged addresses. No one paid any such attention to Bella. Their eyes merely swung by her as though she did not exist. She had kept a steady watch on the news all this time but there had been nothing. She went to a local café and logged onto the internet for the first time in three months and did a search on her name. The first five or so hits were of different people who shared her name.

When she clicked on the last entry, she saw her picture. Except that was a picture of how she had looked before the plastic surgery on her nose, lips and eyes. The person sitting in the next seat would never have recognised her. The hit was a section from a newspaper reporting of how she had been lost overboard during a storm on a South Sea island. Bella knew at once what was going on. In order to get her millions her husband would have to prove that she was dead. They needed it to be in a small island nation so that no proper investigation would be carried out. Her husband was the only beneficiary. She had no other close relations. The item on the net had a quote from Maude who claimed to have witnessed Bella being swept overboard during the storm. Bella had always sensed Maude's jealousy but the degree of cold-blooded calculation was quite awe-inspiring. All Bella's money would go to them unless she acted. Bella spent the following night worrying about what to do next.

When morning came, she did nothing.

There was a path along the cliffs that had a wide view of the Pacific. Bella found herself walking along it. The morning was cold with a sharp wind. It was still very early. She stood on the highest point above the rocks some distance below. Bella felt the last crumb of her will blow out across the cliff's edge.

She didn't notice that an elderly man had moved up beside her.

"Don't do it," he said in a gruff manner. When Bella turned and looked at him, he showed no sign of sympathy. "We're not high enough." He was regarding Bella aggressively as though he was expecting some wounding retort.

The man's name was Darcy Cole; he had spent his life as a clerk for the local council. He lived alone in the house left to him by his mother. He had never lived anywhere else. He was retired and was therefore able to devote all his time to his life-long hobby, which was the study of ancient Rome. He could write in Latin as fluently as in English and he kept up a vigorous correspondence with other scholars around the world, but that was his only contact with the rest of humanity. He could hardly have been more out of place than in a New Zealand farming community and yet he had never left the little town. The few people who thought about it had always assumed he was slightly mad. This may have been unfair when Darcy was a younger man and had looked after his mother devotedly. He had behaved strangely but this could have been put down to severe shyness. Since retiring, however, he had become rude to everyone and evermore strange in his behaviour. The fact was that his memory of recent events was confused. Dementia was eating away at his brain.

"Come," he said, "help me down this hill. There is a lot of dew on the ground, I might slip."

"Of course," answered Bella politely. She could see immediately that he was not totally aware of the world about him.

"You looked like Dido, staring out at the departing Aeneas. Some things never change. *Semper eadem*. Virgil, you know, was far greater than Shakespeare."

As they clambered down the hillside, Darcy told her the complete history of Dido and Aeneas, often lapsing into the language of the original poem. He spoke of these mythical people as if he had just met them at the post office.

He seemed to believe that he knew this woman who was leading him by the arm and that she, in some way, had a duty of care towards him. Perhaps he thought Bella was his nurse. He had been taken to hospital some months previously after he had been found wondering along the main road out of town. Permanent accommodation in a care home had been considered, but Darcy would not hear of it and he did have long periods when he seemed to understand his situation, and so the hospital had reluctantly allowed him to go home.

At his gate that morning he said, "I would like a cup of tea now."

His house was tiny and dark. It smelled musty but not unpleasantly so. It was filled with books of every description, most of which were in Latin. The house was in need of cleaning but the tea was of a high quality. Bella warmed the pot thoroughly and allowed a good five minutes for it to brew.

Once he had settled into one of the floral easy chairs which filled the space in the living room not given over to books, Darcy said, "I seem to have forgotten your name."

Bella began to weep. To her surprise Darcy laid his hand upon hers.

"Whatever is the matter?" he asked. "Tell me about it."

During the long hottest part of the day, Bella told Darcy everything. Far more than she had ever told another living soul. Darcy never interjected and never advised; he seemed to be following what she said.

BELLA LOOKED after Darcy until he died the following year; during his last illness she did indeed become his nurse. During all that time she never seriously considered making any attempt to regain her old life. She settled easily into the community and people were generally accepting and kind towards her.

When Darcy was buried, two professors turned up to the local Catholic parish church where a requiem mass was held by special dispensation in Latin. The priest, who had always been rather in awe of Darcy, gave a very moving address. Several of the older inhabitants of the town were there, people who had known Darcy's family all their lives. Two cousins came hoping for some inheritance and they were indeed the only beneficiaries. After the sale of his books, Darcy's estate amounted to a little more than one hundred thousand dollars.

The local butcher, who had known Darcy for sixty years, asked Bella what she would do.

"I'm going back," she replied.

Bella didn't know what she had become after her life with Darcy, but she knew one thing for certain: she was no longer nothing.

MODERN PAINTERS

1975

THE RED BRICK walls of the old warehouse on the wharf ran down into the grey waters of Auckland Harbour. Steve, the apprentice, stared out through a tiny window across the water and wondered at his fate. His heart raced with the humming excitement of life, while around him the workaday world was dull indeed. In the clear sunlight, he could see across the harbour to an urban landscape that was speckled with manicured volcanos, surrounded by neat little buildings, all square and straight.

Steve was a liar. Life was just too boring as it was; he liked to weave into it some extra colour. He didn't really think of this as lying. He was providing an alternative vision that was more consistent with what he saw in the world about him, not like the cold, fake reality which the white people of New Zealand always insisted upon. His people knew more of the life within life than these prosaic newcomers. But the truth was that they were the dominant people, and he would have to learn to be as flat and as matter-of-fact as them or he'd spend his life with no job.

He had been a year on the job access programme where he

worked for a company but was paid a small amount by the government. He belonged to a paint gang because he had always been good at drawing. The other members of the gang put up with him, but he hadn't been accepted by them.

He studied the squarely built colonial wooden houses across the harbour in Devonport and tried to think along straight lines and smother his imagination. It was still half an hour till lunch time. Tony, Julie and Ron had just finished morning tea. They were working at the new big window.

"Get the tea on, Steve," said Ron.

"It's almost lunch time."

Ron was an experienced tradesman in his fifties. He'd spent the weekend working on his boat so he didn't want to overdo it today.

Julie's radio blared away in its specially made box.

"You know I like Abba, but I don't like them on television."

Julie's statement drifted across the new 'fitness centre' like a dog with a stick. It bounced off the dusty floor, rubbed along the fresh yellow walls and finally gave up all hope of a reply. It was always this way with Julie's efforts at conversation.

"Look out here, eh?" shouted Steve. "There's a girl on a motorboat nude bathing, eh?"

Ron and Tony dashed to the small window and flung Steve aside. Of course, it was a hoax. They chased after the young liar and finally cornered him. Tony threw a brick, which hit the boy's knee. It was a heavy blow, but Steve disguised the fact that they had hurt him.

"Back you dogs," he cried, as he slid off to make the tea.

Tony, the foreman, was always bitter and moody.

He was younger than Ron and Julie but was much less well off than them. His passion was cards.

"No use starting back now. It would be a dead loss. May as well have lunch and get on with the game. Have you got the tea on, Steve? You better have! Lying little creep."

Ron and Julie climbed down and plunged their brushes into

the turps. Tony set up the card table he carried with him on every job. Steve filled the kettle out of the lavatory cistern by way of revenge. He put in the same tea bags he had used for morning tea and boiled them in the kettle.

"That kid's mad," said Tony.

"Always telling lies. You can't believe anything he says. And he can't keep a straight line, you know. He's a bloody hopeless painter. How can anyone be a painter if they can't keep straight lines?"

"I don't know, I'm sure," said Ron, who in a long career had always found it best to agree with the foremen.

"I'll get rid of him, don't you worry." Tony's expression showed real menace.

"Look quite choice in here when it's done." As usual, nobody took any notice of Julie. "Nice pale yellow walls, very nice."

"He thinks he's clever," continued Tony as though Julie hadn't spoken. "But he can't even keep a straight line. He's a mad little creep."

"He's mad, right enough," agreed Ron.

"And then, when the floors are polished and all the training gear moved in, it will be really neat." Julie looked about her, imagining the room after its completion. She ate very little for lunch, but she was very heavily built and was much stronger than the men. Her thin, sandy hair was drawn under an old blue cap. Her face was delicate and freckled. She seemed much younger than Ron, although they were of a similar age.

Ron had a scrawny body, almost as slight as a child's, and yet lined and haggard. He drank much more than was good for him. Tony had employed Ron and Julie for their ability to play bridge. Steve was being 'taught' to make up the four. Tony had asked him if he played when he came for the job and as usual Steve had lied. The two hours of bridge was the only time in the day when Julie would turn off her radio. She was the best player and therefore had Steve as her partner. Tony and Ron were always on the defensive for, despite the handicap of her partner,

Julie usually won, much to Tony's displeasure. Steve was afraid of Tony's anger. Several times, the foreman had lashed out when the boy's attention had wondered. Steve liked to talk; he hated the competition and the playing with numbers.

"Be choice if there was nude bathing, eh? Be choice, eh?"

Tony played far slower than the others, always taking a great deal of time to choose his card. It might have given him an unfair advantage except that he was always too wound up to think clearly. He had no talent for the game despite his obsession with it; he had read a great many books on bidding and play, none of which he had properly understood. He was always giving the others lectures on strategy, which continued even as they defeated him.

Julie had never read a book on cards in her life and never theorised about the game. She simply had the knack of concentrating with great efficiency and her memory of the hands was faultless. Unlike Tony, she played fast, having worked out the lie of the cards after the first few tricks. There was always something faintly impatient about the way in which she regarded the table and seemed to have anticipated every move that was made.

Ron had a good natural feel for the cards but was preoccupied with the cigarettes he was forever rolling and dangling from the corner of his mouth. Steve was always fascinated to watch him draw the lethal smoke into his lungs as if he were forcing some lover into infinite submission and then exhaling in a final gesture of domination. Ron stared at his cards as though it were some irritating chore; his main preoccupation was with the slim white parcel of tobacco smouldering in his hands.

Tony always dealt the first hand; it was one of the many ways he had of forcing the play in his direction and subtly cheating. He handled the cards much as Ron handled his cigarette but without the same authority; despite his best efforts the game would never bend to his will. In the first hand, Steve pretended he had better cards than was the case. He went down badly. But for the rest of the game, Julie and Steve won easily. It put Tony in a wicked mood. After the tenth defeat in a row, he declared the game over even though it was only fifteen minutes past the official start-back time.

Tony was made even more angry shortly after when Eric the boss walked in with two men in business suits. 'Goons', as Tony called them.

"You lot doing OK?" Eric was glad to find them working.

"What have you come for?" answered Tony. "Can't you leave us in peace?"

He glowered at the new arrivals, full of unreasoning hatred.

"Hello," Eric smiled. "Julie in good form again, is she?"

The three men inspected the building without seeming to take much in. Perhaps they were confused by the fact that the job seemed no further on than it had been the week before. Steve liked to watch the men in suits who often came to visit them on the job. He enjoyed seeing how they coped with the guilt of being in a privileged position before the painters in their dirty overalls. Sometimes they feigned a bluff aggressive manner as though they believed themselves quite worthy of their lofty position in life. Others would try to be matey and make weak jokes and talk about the rough life that they used to have. Nothing ever worked; the guilt remained clearly in their faces. Steve did not envy them. Whatever they did he always felt sorry for the white folks with their tight, straight little minds. If only they could relax but that seemed forever beyond them. The suited men stayed longer than usual and filled several pages of notes. Tony expected them to change the colour scheme or something equally typical of the wavering management, but they didn't say anything before leaving. As they were walking out, one of the young executives nodded at Steve and winked at him in a feeble attempt at comradeship. Steve nodded back out of sympathy.

The painters had afternoon tea early to get over the interruption.

"You know," began Julie, "it's really strange, but people

always look like what they do for a living. Those two architects just could not be anything else. They just looked like architects."

Tony was still in a temper. He glowered at Julie and said darkly under his breath, "So you look like a painter, God help us."

Even this was not said to Julie in answer to her idea; it was spoken as though making some remark about a mad person whose presence was somehow less than human.

Julie was hurt, but she was too slow-witted to think of any reply. The pathetic cheerfulness which she maintained was quite broken. Steve was suddenly aware of the shallowness of her confidence and the unhappiness she continually laboured against. He knew it was foolish to cross his foreman in his present mood, but he did so anyway. Even before he spoke, he knew what the consequence would be.

"At least there's one thing you don't look like anyway, Tony, and that's a card player, eh?"

Tony's face became white with rage. "And you will never be a painter!"

Steve didn't show any change in his quiet manner. There was even an edge of sympathy in his voice as he said to Tony without any trace of fear or excitement, "That's all right, man, if you don't want me to come tomorrow you only gotta say, eh?"

"OK then, don't come tomorrow. I've had enough of you."

"That's all right, man. Don't worry about it, I've had enough of this job, anyway."

"I'm not worried. You're the one with the problem. You can never tell the truth."

"Don't get angry, man, I'm going. Look, I'm going now, eh? See ya."

As Steve walked out of the building, he seemed as casual as ever. Tony and Ron set back to work, Julie followed after a short interval. She turned up the volume on her radio. None of them spoke again all afternoon. Tony did some painting himself on the tricky antique window frames, keeping a faultless line, never touching the dusty glass.

The following morning Eric and the two architects of the previous day were waiting outside the building when the gang arrived.

"What you here for?" asked Tony, on guard.

"It's a materials check. These two gentlemen reckon there are certain items missing from the store room they were checking yesterday."

Tony knew this meant trouble. He had constructed a garden shed from the building materials in the store. Ron had taken quite a few things for his boat. Even Julie had taken a few tins of paint.

"Are you calling us thieves?"

"Let's just go and look. You got the key?"

"He won't need it," said Julie who was standing by the door.

"Look the lock's been busted."

Tony couldn't believe his good fortune as he led them inside the fitness centre. But then as they entered the main hall, all six of them stopped in amazement. On the wall opposite, which had been a pale yellow the night before, was a large mural. A swirling array of curving figures, not a detailed drawing but a sweeping evocation of athletic action. It was an astonishing effort for a single night's work.

Steve had his back to them, still painting. "Hey, man," he said without turning round. "What do you think of my straight lines?"

"There's your thief," said Tony.

CHALK

When I was a young student, I lived for some time in England as a lodger in a house overlooking the rolling hills of the chalk downs and the sea. Most days the wind blew from the ocean onto the sturdy two-storey building and I was nearly always bitterly cold in my tiny room. Mine was a corner room over the stairs, a space the same shape as the bed and only a little bigger. There was a desk of the kind you would find in a school room, a metal chair, some paper-thin curtains over the leaky window frames and nothing else. For hours, weeks and months I sat at the desk, staring out at the wind and the sea.

My landlady had lived her whole life on chalk. She used to say it made you healthy. Her husband must have spent some time on other soils for he had died, and she had been forced to take in a student. She was very brave and did not resent me exactly; she treated me as a test of character. She actively supported the Liberal Party. She had three sons of her own; with them she was polite, business-like and totally unemotional. The three boys were very well scrubbed and altogether chalky. She was not blind to their faults. "I'm afraid Rick can be a bit much at times." From this, you will understand that this eldest boy of twenty years was both ignorant and boorish. To me, she was about the same as with her sons, only a little less polite. I was unwelcome but I was endured with great fortitude.

The family was cold and stiff to an extraordinary degree; their whole life was one of form. They were forever thanking each other and making little speeches expressing their gratitude for things that were not really gifts. One day, the youngest boy was sitting on the sofa, something painfully wrong with his big toenail. He was in agony, clutching at a cushion as his mother bound his foot. When she noticed his discomfort, she informed him that a certain amount of crying would be acceptable if he so wished. Only then did he begin to wail.

Her cooking was appalling but meals were consumed with great respectability. She knew how bad it was. "You see, I would much rather be in the garden." Whatever she prepared was sure to be found floating in a little flood of salty, waterlogged, puffy bits of grain. These may have been derived from rice. I have never seen such stuff before or since. Her garden, it must be said, was splendid.

The magnificent white house was one of many detached residences on the side of the downs. There were several tree-lined avenues running in from the coast road. The region was bleak indeed. Most of the time, the cold wind howled into my little room. The hillsides were bare except for a few sheep and the ragged fences enclosing the pasture. Often, the rain came slanting in from the sea. It was not a wild landscape; it was merely an empty one. All flattened down, controlled, clean and, most of all, white.

Twice a day, people would be in evidence: in the morning when they set out for their work and each evening when they returned. They were mostly men in suits; a few sons and daughters in school uniforms. There were, however, some houses that seemed quite deserted. They lay deep in their drives behind the neatly clipped hedges.

Each morning and night, I had to take a long bus ride. It was like entering a world without words to clamber onto the rickety double-deckers, which were blue and cream like milk jugs. Everyone was strictly silent. Occasionally, children would speak; sometimes, they almost shouted and were positively lively, but this was literally frowned upon. The older people behaved as though they were the only people on earth. It was an event if the words 'Excuse me' were exchanged as elbows touched or someone made way for another person. Eyes were never engaged. If one looked inward then it was at the floor; mostly, gazes were fixed through the murky windows at the all-too-familiar streets that lurched by. Most of the people on these buses clearly hated the ride and prayed for it to end. I have never seen people quite so bored and dejected; so sick of their lives.

Two others waited at the bus stop with me each morning for the eight-twenty. One was a neat, well-groomed businessman who wore a suit and a bowler hat. He carried a rolled umbrella and a *Daily Telegraph*. During the journey, he would complete the crossword, which was quite an achievement in the time available. Many the hour I spent staring at his greased hair beneath the rim of his hat or hearing him rustling behind me.

My other fellow traveller at the stop was a French girl, an au pair of eighteen or so. She was slight with masses of red hair and a freckled face. She was always dressed very prettily but modestly. She seemed as shy and afraid as I was. I cannot describe her any further as I would never allow myself to look at her.

Most days as we waited at the stop an elderly lady would charge by as her dog took her for a walk. She wore bizarre clothes of ancient fashions and bright colours, heavy masculine shoes and thick stockings. She was always cheery and actually smiled at us as she went by. I always returned her smile as warmly as I could and even thought of saying good morning, but I was never able to raise the courage. I believe the French girl also returned her smile, but *Daily Telegraph* was invariably lost in his crossword.

The lady with the dog was the person I knew and liked best

in this Downside village even though we had never exchanged a word. We were both great walkers on the downs. The little white trails led through the tall grass in every direction. I would follow these paths every day, terribly depressed by the extreme loneliness of this English world. The dramatic sweep of the bare white hills was somehow uncertain and, if anything, increased my despondency. Anyone that I met would invariably avoid acknowledging my presence and would very often change their direction in order to avoid meeting me. Once, I came upon an accident on the downs; a young girl had been kicked in the face after falling from her horse. I tried to help, but she made it clear that she did not want any help from me and despite the concussion and the pain, she preferred to lead her mount back to the village alone. Some instinct seemed to preclude any contact with me despite the state she was in. If I am honest, I must admit that I was glad not to be involved.

The one person who didn't shun me was the lady with the dog. She would come bounding along, leaning back against the weight of her dog. She would nod and smile her smile, which conveyed a complicity between us. It seemed to say, "Yes, this is a crazy, lifeless way of living but at least you and I know that it is; at least, we wish for something better." I imagined her living alone with one of those great houses all to herself. I felt sure that the place must be deliciously messy and full of interesting things like fine pictures or the remnants of her dead father who had been, I felt sure, a military man.

One morning, a great event occurred at the bus stop. The bus did not arrive! The businessman simmered almost perceptibly, and the French girl was more demure than ever. Suddenly, high along the road, we heard a shrill whistling. The lady with the dog was positively running towards us, tooting away on her police whistle.

Daily Telegraph, to my amazement, shouted to her as soon as she was within earshot. "Dora, whatever is it? Do stop blowing that whistle."

Despite the way he had completely ignored her when she passed each morning, the two were obviously related.

"I am sorry, John, dear," answered Dora who was evidently his wife or sister. "But the bus has broken down. You'll have to walk along to the coast road."

"Really, Dora, are you mad?" John's voice was clear and resonant; it was like an actor's.

Dora was obviously very used to his childish rudeness. I decided wife was more likely than sister.

He strode harshly away before she reached the stop. She was left looking after him. Her dog was pulling after the man but she, for once, resisted all motion. It was then that she gave me a smile, her smile of alliance. Her bravery raised my spirits higher than they had been for months.

We three commuters walked the windy half mile or so to the coast road in silence. I looked towards the French girl and in my elation began to smile at her. I might even have spoken but for her look of horror that I might do such a thing.

That look confirmed that she, along with so many of these white people, wanted nothing to do with a black man.

THE YELLOW AND THE GREEN

I think it was the yellow and the green. Fresh colours like spring. As you can see, they're everywhere. Perhaps that's all it takes to attract a stranger of no fixed abode with money in his pocket.

Money, money to burn. Not that I saw it like that, not then, not when I came here. I acquired these funds by legal means, I should add. Ten years in Saudi Arabia is legal in the extreme. I had a rich uncle who told me that such a time in the Middle East would be the making of me. Well, I suppose it was.

Twenty-one to thirty-one might not be the formative years, but they are the time when one is made or unmade. Ten years of tedious, brutal endeavour. No booze, no family, nothing but work. Yes, they made me.

Now here. The southern seas. Where the green and the yellow dance in the warm air, on the flowers, in the bush, in the sea, in the eyes of the women. Here is the antithesis of Arabia. Escape.

It was expensive but, yes, that house on the beachfront is mine. I bought it in cash. This is even my bit of beach. Not that I would ever keep anyone off it. This is my garden of yellow and green, growing like crazy. More colour than I saw in ten years in the other place.

And yes, this is my Jarana. She often wears hibiscus in her hair for me with its green stem and a heart of pure gold. She's even a good cook and so gentle. Like that warm breeze off the sea each day. Gentle like the breath of God.

And, now can't you guess? Ah, yes, I can see in your eyes that you can. I leave for Riyadh on Thursday.

THE SPINNEY

1960

HER GRANDSON TOMMY was doing very well for himself. As Sarah waited at her window for him and his family, just the thought of him made her happy. Sarah had a conviction that this was what could be done if the people in a family love each other; the peace it brings spreads out. He had been such a clever little boy, so full of ideas and so good with people. He seemed almost too kind for his own good, but there was strength there too; he always knew what he wanted and nearly always got it. Sarah had no idea where his sense of duty came from, but when he was small, he would come to see her twice a week. He knew what a difference it would make to her widowed existence. She would make him tea in his favourite yellow cup and then they would play dominoes. This had gone on right up until his teenage years. Doing thoughtful, kind things seemed to come naturally to him as it did to his parents.

Now Tommy was a married man with two little girls of his own; he was well qualified and had a good job yet he still thought of her and came to see her often.

Sarah was at her window because they were all going to take

her for a drive, and they would have a picnic. What a treat. Her heart was feeling good today. On good days she felt like new. She had never expected to last so long; she had been a widow for far more years than she had been married.

ONCE IN THE car her two great-granddaughters got her to tell them again the story of the dominoes and how their father enjoyed the pattern of the tiles more than winning the game and all the other worn-out tales that made them laugh no matter how many times they were repeated.

She had told Tom and his wife, Ann, that these years, while their children were small, would be the best of their life. It was so typical of them that they understood this remark completely and agreed with it. She had come to see that it is so rare for people to get things right, but when they do as with Tom and Ann, everything seems so easy.

Soon they were on their way, with Sarah sitting beside Tom in the front seat. He was already driving quite quickly, travelling east out of the city, before he asked, "So then, Grandma, where shall we go? You can choose."

"Oh, I don't know. So much has changed, nowhere seems real to me any more."

"What about Swadlincote, where you grew up?"

"Oh, I don't know about that, I don't think I could bear it. It's too sad."

"There are no mines there any more, it's all been swept away. There are just massive fields with piles of bricks and concrete slabs. You could look at your old house and we could have a picnic on the spinney."

It was clear that this was where he wanted to go.

"There's so much history there. You can tell us all about it. You must have some lovely memories. I want the girls to see where they come from."

How can I bear it? thought Sarah, but how could she refuse him? They were being so kind. She did not say anything more and so it was that the car headed out through the villages that led into Derbyshire and the scene of her childhood.

In less than half an hour they were on the very road where the most wonderful event of her life had happened, and before she knew it they were at the very junction. The pattern of the roads had stayed in her mind all these years.

Sarah wanted to ask Tom to slow down but she didn't. In a flash they had passed the place. She had tried to take it in, but they were travelling far too quickly. From what she could tell it hadn't changed at all. There were still the high hedges on both sides of the road and the lane was just as narrow. How many times had she dreamed of that narrow stretch of tarmac that had always seemed somehow temporary, as though it would be pulled up one day soon only for the grass to grow again. But it was seventy years ago, and the place was just the same. Their rescue might have happened yesterday.

Tommy, with his sharp mind and uncanny sense of direction, soon found the village street where she had lived with her mother and Bill James. He hadn't been there since he was a child, but he knew exactly where the short terrace of miners' cottages had been.

"They've gone," he said, slowing to a stop. "Look at that. Not a trace."

Sarah believed that this was the right spot, but she recognised nothing. In her memory the street was all closed in and dark, now there was space and open sky everywhere. Across the road, where the pit gates and workings had been, there was just a tall wire fence behind which was a huge expanse of debris, just piles of bricks and stone running off into the distance. She was not filled with sadness as she had expected to be because there was nothing that was even remotely familiar. Tom was quite a bit deflated.

"Oh well," he said, "let's go to the spinney. Why on earth

would they knock everything down and not put anything in its place?"

As they travelled out of the village there were some cottages that Sarah thought she recognised but they were going by too quickly for her to be sure.

The spinney was also much changed; it was far better kept than in Sarah's day, when it had just been a stretch of waste ground leading up to a small hill crowned with a stand of poplar trees. Now it was a park with lawns and a playground. Tom pulled into the car park and they helped Sarah across to a bench beside the path that led up the hill. She remembered running up to the top and playing hide and seek with her sister. It had been twenty years since her sister Netty had died. Sarah steered her mind away from that thought.

Tom was soon racing the girls to the top of the spinney. He was such a good dad. She had always known he would be.

"Are you OK?" asked Ann with real concern. "Tom was going to come here whatever you said. His mind was set on it. I don't think he understands nostalgia."

"Oh, yes, I'm fine thank you, Ann. I feel much better than expected. It's all so changed, it may as well be a different place. I remember this though, the spinney. My sister Netty and I would come here and play all day. We would not think of going home until dark."

"What was her real name? I've never heard of a Netty."

"It was Janet. All Janets were Netty in those days."

"Was your father a miner?"

"No. Well, it depends what you mean by father."

Sarah considered how much to tell her granddaughter-in-law. She knew that unless she did, no one would ever know about Bill James and his kindness miracle. She had never told her son, Tom's father. She had been too ashamed, but things were changing now; no one in the modern world would blame her for the sins of her father.

Ann was looking at her closely, expecting her to go on and so she did. It would be quite a while before Tom and the kids come down from the spinney.

"My real father was a drunk and a wife-beater. He never did any work for as long as he lived, and he did live for a long time. I never really knew him. I never even saw him once we walked out, and that was when I was ten. I remember him though. I reckon that the kind of fear you have as a child is worse than anything you go through as a grown-up. And, my God, I feared that man. The worse times were when he got some money. He would come home drunk and beat us up. My mother would take in washing and clean people's houses just to feed us, but sometimes he would steal her savings and then he would come home the worst for wear and start on my mother."

Sarah stopped at this point and tried to assess if she should go on. Ann seemed so innocent and she came from quite a genteel background. Perhaps she didn't want to hear any more of this, perhaps she would think less of Tom. Her expression seemed pained more than anything.

"How dreadful. How did you get away from him?"

"Netty and I were going to murder him. One night we waited at the bottom of the stairs with a carving knife but we both fell asleep!"

Sarah laughed as she said this, which to Ann seemed inconceivable, but the laugh was from some deep inner store of strength which is able to see the absurd in even the most ghastly of circumstances. It made Ann realise just how formidable Sarah must have been to have survived all this.

"When we woke up it was all over. My mother was a mass of blood and bruises, and he was passed out on the bed. The next morning, really early, when it was just light and the birds were singing, my mother cleaned us all up as best she could, put on our best clothes and we walked out of the house. All we took was a small leather satchel. We couldn't carry anything else. We were so small and mother was in such a bad way."

Sarah said this without any sadness in her voice; it was as if she was describing something ordinary.

"But where did you go?"

"That was it; that was the awful part about it. My mother didn't have a single friend in the village. No one wanted to be associated with us. There is prejudice and snobbery at every level of life. People were so disgusted by my father they ostracised the whole family.

"We turned down the lane towards this village. Thank God that we did. We walked for what must have been a couple of hours. There really was nowhere for us to go, and my mother was on the point of collapse. We reached the lane we came down this morning. I recognised it just now. It hasn't changed. I even know the exact place where we were saved."

Sarah stopped for a few moments; that morning long ago was obviously still vivid in her mind. Soon she continued on, pausing now and then as if to make the telling of the story take up the same amount of time as the events.

"Netty was very small and my mother had to pick her up. We were all almost done but then like a miracle we heard a pony and trap coming up behind us. It pulled up level with us and stopped. The sun was behind the man in the trap so I couldn't see him properly, but I could see a black moustache and I could see that he was a big fella."

"I saw that my mother daren't look at him. She kept her eyes looking down the road. Her poor face was all puffy with yellow and purple patches, it was heartbreaking."

"The man looked down on us for what seemed like ages although it was probably only a moment. The horse then began to get restless as though it wanted to be away. I think we all expected him just to drive on. He didn't; he settled the horse down and then he said, 'Step up here, m'dear.'

"Only then did my mother turn her face towards him. For a moment she was still, and I suppose in any other circumstances she would have hesitated or at least said something but after no more than a few seconds she handed Netty up to him and climbed up into the bench seat. She pulled me up, and I sat between them. He handed Netty back into my mother's arms and drove on. He never said another word until we were in the village and outside his house. He took us into his front room and then went to get Florrie, a neighbour, who did her best to attend to my mother.

"Can you imagine what might have become of us had he not come along that lane on that Sunday morning? As it was he who took us in. His name was Bill James, he was six feet two and yet he still went down the mine for his whole life. He was the most good-natured person I have ever come across. I feel that everything good in my life, and even Tom's life, rests on his kindness. I lived in his house until I left home to get married. Bill and my mother lived as man and wife until she died. Bill was ten years younger than she was. He was my real father; the other one never came near us."

Ann had received so much more than she had bargained for. The image of Sarah's mother's life was too painful for her to contemplate. She did not want to think about it.

Sarah could see that it was better to change the topic of their conversation. Cruelty and meanness in all its forms were still all around, just as they would always be. What was the point of digging for it in the past? She was glad she had told someone however, for now at least for a little time longer, the kindness of Bill James would be remembered.

They were silent for some time. Ann could not formulate a suitable way of reacting to such revelations. Tom and his giggling little daughters were already starting down towards them. Sarah could swear that his features resembled those of Bill James.

"I've got a pork pie in my bag," she said. "Tom used to love them."

THE MASTERCLASS

"Your fingernails sound like bread knives."

Marion's guitar fell silent. Her face was filled with desperation.

"But I've been working on them for hours."

In fact, she had completely forgotten her nails. She was so nervous she could hardly remember her name.

"It just won't do," continued Mrs Carter. "This man is one of the best five classical guitarists in the world. *In the world!* I'm not exaggerating. What is he going to think of me as a teacher when he hears you?"

Marion did not reply and looked like she was near tears. Jill Carter relented.

"Here, give me your hand."

The elderly woman took Marion's hand in hers and began to work upon the four most important fingers. First, with the finest grade of sandpaper and then with the soft patch of leather she always carried with her.

"You'll be all right. You always do well in performance. You won't let me or yourself down. I wouldn't have chosen you otherwise, now would I?"

She was actually being kind. Marion had never experienced

that before. The white-haired, sparkly-eyed teacher was the best in town, but usually she was also the angriest.

"Don't work any more now. I know you're going to play like an angel. Believe me, I know it."

She tried to say this lightly but they both knew how rare it was for Jill Carter to praise anyone. There was something in her eyes that made Marion aware of just how much the teacher believed in her. It had the most wonderful calming effect. Suddenly the nerves were gone. Instead of wishing she were a thousand miles away, she now felt sure of herself. Instead of dreading the next few minutes, she found herself looking forward to them. It meant that she could relax and concentrate.

Mrs Carter continued. "To tell you the truth, I have never liked masterclasses. A lesson in public can never do anyone any good. But the entire musical community will be out there tonight. That's what a big name can do. And a recommendation from Michel Colberg could get you into anywhere; the Royal College in London, the Juilliard in New York, anywhere."

There was a knock on the door; it was one of the TV stage managers.

"Five minutes, Marion."

MICHEL COLBERG, in his dressing room, felt infinitely tired. This was the third leg of a round-the-world tour and the demands upon his physical and nervous energy were enormous. To become one of the best was hard enough but to maintain that position was harder still. Audiences expected to be delighted and amazed by his technical skill and musicality. It was hard to turn this on every night when living out of strange hotel rooms on even stranger food. Everyone always expected him to be so kind. He had always tried to impress and be charming and find time for private lessons and masterclasses. He felt that it was his duty to do them and that it was right to share the magic of his talent and learning, especially in out-of-the-way places such as New Zealand. It was his first trip to this country, and he had been surprised at the interest and excitement his visit had created. His recital at the Aotea Centre that evening was to be broadcast nationwide on the national classical music radio channel. He tried not to think of the thousands of people who would be listening to every sound he made. It was a very bad piece of scheduling to have a masterclass on the afternoon before a concert but he felt he should be accommodating to the local enthusiasts.

In the recital hall, which was filled with many local dignitaries and the artistic cognoscenti, the president of the Music Society made his speech. He explained how hard it was for both pupil and teacher in the masterclass situation and how grateful they all were to Mr Colberg for giving his time when he had to perform that evening. He finished with a tedious list of local events. On one side of the stage Michel waited, trying to look the part, hoping the students would not be too awful. It was always such a trial if they played badly and he had to find some diplomatic way of saying so. He would never lie to a pupil; he took his art far too seriously for that.

On the other side of the stage he could see the first student waiting, guitar in hand. She was a girl of about twenty. She had an intelligent expression about her dark eyes and a surprising calmness. There was an air of defiance in her poise. Michel was impressed by such composure on such a trying occasion.

Marion had spotted Maestro Colberg the instant he appeared in the wings. He had the reputation among guitarists as the most handsome man in the profession. She had gazed at his pictures a thousand times but in person he didn't look like any of them. He had a strong Nordic face and blond, almost white, hair which flopped down over one eye. He exuded relaxed elegance. Suddenly he began walking towards her, and Marion realised she was about to be called onto the stage.

Michel was not an extrovert and found the beginning of all

appearances difficult. It was one of the many contradictory things about him. He was a shy man and yet he gave solo performances each evening in crowded auditoriums. He had a large and powerful body and yet his classical guitar playing was of infinite delicacy and elegance. He was born to a family of physicians and yet from the very beginning he had shown the unmistakable qualities of an artist. He began by addressing the audience directly.

"Ladies and gentlemen. Thank you for joining us this afternoon. I hope our lessons will prove enjoyable for everyone. I have devoted my life to the guitar, and I consider it an honour as well as a duty to do what I can to help new players."

What an arrogant thing to say, thought Marion. *He's hardly thirty himself and he talks as though he were Segovia.*

"And so, without further ado" — Michel's English had just a hint of his native Sweden — "I would like to introduce Marion, the first musician to play for us today."

He raised his arm theatrically and welcomed Marion onto the stage. She walked to the centre of the platform to where the stool and music stand were set out and, without smiling, bowed crisply to the encouraging applause. Michel watched her closely. The fact that Marion had not smiled was very significant to him. He had always felt that there was something in a smile which betrayed a performance into triviality. Once when he had played in Jakarta, he had been asked, "Why do Westerners laugh at great music?" and had been thanked for not grinning. Marion showed not a trace of fear or embarrassment and seemed quite self-possessed. Yet he found himself going into his masterclass routine of trying to calm his pupil.

"Please, come and sit down. How do you feel?"

What an inane question, thought Marion. *He expects me to say that I feel nervous.*

"Good," said Marion. "I feel good."

Michel, by biting his tongue, was just able to avoid saying

"Not nervous?" Instead he managed, "And what are you going to play for us this afternoon?"

Marion looked him squarely in the eyes and said, "*Sevilla*, Albéniz."

Michel felt his spirits drop. *Sevilla* was one of the Pictures of Spain, opus 46 by the great Spanish pianist Albéniz. The piece was extraordinarily difficult to play on the piano and only the most skilful virtuosi had been able to play a guitar transcription. Amateurs usually played it very badly or they simplified it until it became a very shallow reflection of its true self. The music must evoke a carnival of sound with flamenco dancers on a fire-lit Spanish night. It was not just a dance; it was a celebration of the dance of life. To do all that on guitar requires special talent. Michel thought it very unlikely that Marion was possessed of such talent and thought it foolhardy to attempt such a work.

"That is a very tough piece," he said, his insincerity seeping through. "You are very brave." He turned to the audience. "*Sevilla*, ladies and gentlemen. All light and fire! Please, Marion. Play when you are ready."

Marion waited a long time before beginning. She knew that it was essential that she collect her emotions and concentrate her mind. She blocked out the audience, the great Michel Colberg, all thought of where she was and who she was. She had no thought of technique or all the hours of practice. All she allowed to exist in her world was the music; for her, there were no plucked strings and vibrating chords; there was just the spirit of *Sevilla*. Her beautiful face showed extraordinary strength and determination.

Michel could see that she had tremendous presence. She pitched into the opening flamenco stamping rhythm at a terrific speed, as fast as any pianist would attempt. Michel could not stop himself from flinching at such a daring opening, but he knew that having begun at that rate she would have to maintain it, which would not be easy once the difficult passages arrived. No flamenco dancer ever looked more passionate than did

Marion as the piece unfolded. She had the straight-backed, noble air of a Spanish dancer and was, at once, fearsome and magnificent. The central slow section was taken daringly slow as the opening had been unusually fast and was again filled with pure feeling. Michel found that he had to divide his concentration into two spheres; one listening to the sound and one glorying in her presence, which showed such fearlessness and distinction.

The audience hardly waited for the last note to die before breaking into ecstatic applause. This was just what Michel was afraid of; it had been a very fiery performance but there was much work needed. The technique that Marion had been taught was way off track. She would never play cleanly with a pure sound unless she went right back to basics and relearned from the beginning. She did have her own sound, that individual voice without which no one can hope to become a soloist, but this alone was not enough.

He joined in the applause and smiled his congratulations while desperately thinking of how to say what he had to say.

Finally, the noise subsided.

"How do you feel?" he asked.

"Neat," said Marion, who knew she had played as never before. "I feel really neat."

"First of all, I must compliment you for your courage, and for the commitment you put into your playing. I asked for fire and that is exactly what you gave us."

Marion knew already that he was not entirely pleased with her.

"But you changed many things. You must explain to me why you have changed so many things."

Michel methodically pointed out all the missed notes and changed harmonies; he demonstrated how sections of the piece were supposed to sound and watched as Marion's face fell into disappointment. She tried to respond to his questions but could not and did not want to change her instinctive approach for his fastidious nit-picking. He constantly referred to Spain, a place as remote for her as the far side of the moon.

Michel considered asking her to try the proper fingering, but he knew her technique was not up to it. He felt that poor teaching lay behind the many faults in the performance but the absurd code of politeness between music teachers made it impossible for him to say so. The fact that the audience had been pleased hung in the air like a noose into which Michel had put his head. The very building seemed to challenge, "How dare you be so cruel when she played so well?"

Marion became nervous and tongue-tied. The masterclass had turned into a nightmare. Michel saw that there was no redeeming the situation.

"Thank you for a terrifically passionate performance. You have a wonderful feel for the music."

The look on Marion's face as he said this appalled him, but he could not let her think that instinct was all that was needed to make a musician. *Sevilla* was, for him, a sacred piece of Spanish art and it should not be played without due regard for all that this implied.

MARION WALKED STRAIGHT OUT of the theatre and threw her guitar into the back of her little Japanese car and drove straight home to the old building in Mt Eden where she was flatting. She would have to go to the concert that evening, and she had been asked by the committee of the Music Society to the dinner afterwards, but all she wanted to do with the rest of her afternoon was lie on her bed and that is exactly what she did.

It was some time before she realised that she was crying. She felt utterly exhausted and as she fell off to sleep, her last thought was thank God her mother had not been there to witness this crushing defeat. Thank God she was still in Timaru and knew nothing of this hateful masterclass and how Jill Carter had tricked her into making a fool of herself. Not for a moment did she consider whether what Michel Colberg had said was true or not. Indeed, she hardly remembered his words; she had felt his disapproval rather than heard it. The more she thought of the kind concern in his exquisite eyes and how gently he was trying to let her down, the more she hated him. The telephone rang three times during the afternoon. Marion ignored it.

ONCE THE MASTERCLASS was over and all the students had been dealt with, Michel Colberg had never in his life felt less like giving a concert. All he could think of was the girl he had heard first and how deeply her spirit had touched him. Like so many artistic people, he was insecure. He was in the business of feeling strong emotions and expressing them. Inevitably, he was disturbed by what was happening around him and he was never sure that he had acted properly. He began to feel that he had let his fatigue defeat his instinct. Had he been fair? Did cultural authenticity matter a damn when Spain was twelve thousand miles away? Was not Marion's playing far closer to the centre of what art is all about than anything he was doing on this concert tour of machine-like performances?

For the first time, it struck him that perhaps he had been the pupil instead of the master and that he was the one who had learned most.

There was a tap on his dressing room door. He tried to reassemble his charming 'artist on tour' manner as he moved to answer it.

"I am so sorry to bother you, Mr Colberg. My name is Jill Carter; the committee has assigned me to look after you this afternoon. We have laid on a light meal at about six if that would be suitable."

"No, no thank you, I never eat before a show, but thank you anyway."

"I will be in the bar out in the foyer if you need anything. I don't suppose you will."

"Orange juice, and chocolate, for the interval. That's all ... but wait, I'll come out with you. I don't feel like being alone."

Jill scurried up to the foyer level and commandeered a secluded corner seat. They sat behind their drinks, silent for a moment and then they both started to talk at once. Michel deferred and insisted his companion speak first.

"Actually, Mr Colberg, there is something I would like to ask you but please if it would disturb your concentration ..."

"My programme is fixed in my fingers, Mrs Carter. On tour, one has to be able to take disturbances."

"Well, it was about my pupil, Marion Tui; the first one you heard this afternoon. I think her the most gifted student ever to come my way. I wonder what impression she made upon you?"

He had been alerted by some instinct what her question was going to be. He had been about to try to find out more about Marion himself, but asked this question by a teacher, it was his duty as a professional to remain detached.

"There is something there, certainly, but the technique has to be taken apart."

"Marion has been with me for just three months. Before that, she was self-taught."

Michel found this revelation simply astonishing. He had thought the performance he had witnessed had been the product of years of work and had criticised it on that basis. How unfair he had been, how cruel. He was speechless for a moment. Jill felt it necessary to fill the silence.

"I have not touched her technique for fear of putting out the fire, as it were. She learnt *Sevilla* by ear from your recording."

"I had no idea. What a monster she must think me."

MARION DRAGGED herself out of bed. She had not eaten all day and now she was famished. All there was to eat were some soft corn flakes and a black banana. She went back to bed and ate this mixture and felt even worse. She might have decided not to go to the concert at all but there, at the bottom of her bed, was Colberg's CD cover. His picture looked out at her and she realised that she could never entirely hate him. There was an innocence in his eyes and that touching gentle intelligence. She went to the bathroom, showered and plaited her long, jet-black hair, winding a white satin ribbon into it. She tried seven outfits before deciding upon a simple white dress, the only dress that she possessed. She did not want to be casual at a dinner with all those important people of the music world. There was something about the line of the dress which tonight she found pleasing. The white dress and the white ribbon made a dramatic contrast with her black hair and brown skin. She had never worn make-up, but she had bought some especially for this evening. The violet eye shadow, blusher and red lipstick took half an hour to get right. It was already after seven when she was finally ready and walked out of her untidy room.

She hated the car park under the Aotea Centre and never went there on her own, which meant that she was ages finding a park and had to walk the length of Queen Street before climbing the steps up to the Aotea megalith. The buskers were at work, and Marion felt far more part of their world than part of the flash Aotea set, but there was something about this man Colberg that drew her into the massive impersonal concert hall so full of educated pretentious people.

She was late. She had to stand at the back for the entire first half. By the time she made it to her seat beside Jill Carter the lights had gone down, and the applause was starting for Michel's reappearance. She had not liked what he had played up till that point; it was all modern squeaks and bangs and Michel had played coldly in an effort to fill the Aotea's vastness.

They were only four rows back from the front and as soon as he began the first piece, Michel lifted his eyes from his left-hand fingering and looked to her seat. He saw her at once and from that moment he was playing for her. She did not feel embarrassed for she lost all sense of where she was. The music and the expression in his eyes fascinated her and nothing existed but the meeting of their spirits. She did not know what he played. As each piece ended, everyone, except Marion, applauded. She found that she could not move.

Then the applause was lasting longer, and she realised that it was over and that he was not going to play any more. Only then, she began to clap and cheer, begging for an encore, along with the rest of the audience.

Michel held his hand up for silence.

"Ladies and gentlemen, thank you, thank you with all my heart for your attention and your appreciation. My concert tonight has been very ... very hard for me, for this afternoon ... I am not going to play an encore for you. But you are going to hear something much better than that; something you would have to be deaf not to love, not to feel ..." He paused. The hall was silent.

"Sometimes, all of us are made deaf, we do not hear what it is most important to hear; this afternoon I was like that." He looked at Marion and held out his hand to her. "Marion, please show that you forgive me and play for us all. Play for us all, now."

The audience was frozen. Jill Carter looked absolutely terrified.

"I tried to warn you," she whispered into the silence.

Marion had already risen and was moving to the stage. Michel held his famous guitar out to her. It felt like a beautiful child in her arms.

Marion leant over the strings and began to play.

THE TENT

1966

TERRY SLID across the road with the grace of a ballet dancer. He did four neat pirouettes in the hunched position and dropped out of view into the ditch. His head popped up immediately, like a startled rabbit seeking out predators. He was looking for his bike. The Gold Star, despite its famed handling qualities, had simply slid away from him. The road was dry, but his line through the roundabout had been far too tight.

Arthur, just behind, had enjoyed the performance immensely. He hauled his mate out, singing, "I went sliding round on my arse, I went sliding round on my arse."

"Bleddy hell!" answered Terry, who had a wonderful way with words. "Bleddy, bleddy, bleddy hell!"

They were well over halfway there. The long straights of the Norfolk countryside simply begged to be eaten up by the gleaming machines. Their bark could be heard for miles across the lowland plains. The two had gone steadily quicker as they had become more inured to the speed and the infinite freedom of the wide horizon. Most unusually there was no wind. The ride had become more and more dreamlike as each shallow curve was sucked under the wheels only to reveal another empty stretch as far as the eye could see. They felt a power of concentrated vitality that made all the rest of existence dull indeed. Two hours of this left a drunk, tingling sensation even when dismounting normally.

After falling off, Terry was shaking badly. His physical discomposure did not disturb his affections, however. Naturally his first thought was for the Goldstar, which was still only about a quarter paid for. The footrest was bent and there were serious scratches on the petrol tank, but there was nothing to make the machine unrideable. They hauled the machine upright and switched off the petrol.

Terry was deftly kicking the parts back into place when a family in a Vauxhall Cresta slowed and gawped at them as it swept around the roundabout. The car was pulling a vast caravan about the size of a tennis court. The family made no offer of help, nor was one desired or expected. The two lads were aware, however, of two very attractive teenage sisters in the back of the car. They were smiling ironically, if not provocatively. There was an allure in their look from the back of their dad's Cresta that the lads found indecent.

They still made Yarmouth in under three hours.

"What's that, a tablecloth?" Terry was looking at a light blue square of material that Arthur had thrown on their little patch of camping ground grass. "Why did you bring a tablecloth?"

Arthur seemed a little hurt. "That's the tent," he said, trying to make it sound as though this should have been obvious to even the dull mind of someone unable to negotiate a traffic island. He did not sound convincing. The longest dimension of the tent was less than the height of either man. It had been part of a cowboy and Indian outfit Arthur had received for his tenth birthday. It had been too small then.

It was early in the season and the town was not too crowded. The sky was blue and the air warm. Even the tide was in. Beside the North Sea this counts for much as often the ocean recedes so far as to become barely visible. The two lads walked along the front between the sea and the holiday town. They had only seen the ocean a few times and its presence made for great excitement. The tawdry white buildings advertised amusements in a way they found gaudy but attractive. The fair rang out its promise of pleasure. The sense of release from working life was almost overwhelming although naturally they affected an air of vague indifference.

They were making in the direction of the pier, still in their riding boots and jackets. Terry was tall and thickset with greased black hair. He had been working for some time on his mean look. It was coming on a treat. Arthur was much smaller with wavy brown hair and a peculiar walk which was common to all the members of his large family. He moved with an absolutely straight back and mincing short steps. It was as though the top half and the rest of his body did not really belong together. At home, Terry worked as a builder's labourer while Arthur worked in his father's machine shop. Arthur was the more thoughtful of the two, not that this mattered in the society in which they found themselves. They had been friends since early childhood.

They discovered a good chip shop on this first outing and lay on the grass beside the boating lake. The steps up onto the boat were rickety and there was a good chance of seeing someone fall in.

The fish and chips were spectacular. Every locality surely has something of which it can be proud. There must always be some facet of experience which is vivid and life enhancing even if it is some very small thing. But Terry and Arthur were hardly aware of the pure white cod they ate beside the boats that day. Food had never counted for much in their world. It was unlikely they would ever get a sense of how good it was.

Arthur, who was always the more alert of the two, saw Stephanie and Trina queuing by the little shed where the paddle boats were hired. They were staying together in a boarding house. At home, Stephanie sewed uppers to the soles of shoes and Trina was a trimmer; it was their first time away together. They wore brightly coloured frocks that were too old for them and far too much make-up. They spoke to each other in loud voices and their manner was at once self-conscious and daring. They kept looking towards the grass bank and then looking away again as they saw themselves noticed. They would disguise the turn of their head by pretending to shake out their hair.

"Come on," said Arthur, smashing his chip paper into a ball.

They joined the queue. Terry was much better at meeting girls. His technique was to stare hard at them and after this display of subtlety he would cut to the chase.

"What you looking at?"

"You, what's your name?"

"What's it to you?"

"Wanna go out with you."

Terry and Arthur paid for the boat ride, the rides on the fair, the drinks in the pub; in short, everything. The tide had gone out by the evening and they walked on the beach under a bright moon. The hard sand lay in ripples under their feet. There were miles of moonlit sand to stroll across. As they were nearing the pier, Trina said, "That's where we're staying."

Before either of the lads could say a word, they called out "Night" and they were gone.

Arthur and Terry walked back to the camp talking gloomily of how much of their budget was left.

Terry growled, "Five quid, that cost us five quid" to the stars several times as they stumbled over the sand dunes. It turned into a mournful refrain as they tripped over the sandy grass into the park.

The gap which had been empty beside their patch of grass was now filled by a huge caravan. Parked behind it was the Vauxhall Cresta that had passed them at the scene of Terry's ballet performance.

It had been decided Arthur would sleep in his tent, even though he was too big for it, and Terry had suggested leaning the two bikes together and sleeping in the gap underneath. He was just about to slide himself underneath when someone very close by spoke.

"Are you all right?"

Then followed another voice.

"You didn't hurt yourself, did you?"

The two sisters from the Cresta were on the step of the caravan.

"Bugger me," said Terry, who was never at a loss for a witty rejoinder.

"He's all right," remarked Arthur, his head poking out from his tent. "He just slid off, that's all."

"Would you like to come in for a cup of coffee?" asked one sister in a clear well-spoken voice.

They wore simple white shirts and shorts. They wore no make-up at all. They were very pretty and there was no doubt about it, they had class, a shade too much class for the two boys.

"Mum and Dad are out at the show."

The two boys looked at each other without speaking.

"We won't bite," said one sister with a friendly smile.

An unspoken idea floated in the air between the two boys; it might be summed up as *We do not belong in the world of caravans and BBC pronunciation*. Arthur said, "It's OK, we're tired, you know, long journey and everything. Thanks anyway."

"It's all right," said the sisters as they closed the door of the caravan. "Perhaps another time."

The next morning was spent providing more treats for

Stephanie and Trina. As a consequence, their money was almost gone. They had to keep enough for petrol on the way home.

"Well," said Terry, who felt the appropriate moment had arrived, "do you want to come up onto the dunes with us then?"

"Oh no," answered Stephanie. "Actually we're meeting someone at the fair. We better go or we'll be late. See ya."

When they got back to the campsite, someone had stolen the tent.

"Must be bleddy midgets," said Terry.

There was nothing for it but to go home. They were packing what little they had left and putting on their crash helmets when around the end of the caravan came the two sisters carrying tennis rackets.

"Hi," they said. This was not considered an acceptable greeting by the two men, so they merely nodded and Arthur kick-started his Tiger Cub.

One the sisters shouted something, but they couldn't hear. Arthur stopped his engine.

"Will you give us a ride on your bikes? Mum and Dad are playing golf."

"We could go up onto the dunes," the other said. "Mess around a bit, you know."

Terry had no doubt that he spoke for them both when he gave his succinct reply.

"Piss off," he hissed as he kicked the Goldstar into life.

They stopped at a layby near Norwich to share a tablet of chewing gum, which was all they had left to eat.

"An egg and bacon sandwich," said Arthur. "That's what I could do with now."

The two of them sucked on their gum and watched the traffic rush by. They were sitting on a railway embankment and suddenly there appeared, massive above them, a steamer pulling a goods train. The noise was very close and oppressive. The goods wagons seemed to go on forever. When the train had finally passed it became completely silent again. Even the traffic had ceased.

"Bleddy tennis rackets," said Terry to no one in particular. Suddenly they were both cheerful. Eager to be off, they climbed onto their machines.

The Goldstar and the Tiger Cub sang through the yellow fields of summer.

IN TRANSIT

He didn't seem out of place; indeed he performed his duties on the sea front with a practised assurance. There was, however, something strange about him; something didn't quite add up. Anyway, one night I invited him for a drink. I was surprised how open he was with me and how, in that soft educated voice, he willingly told me his story. I'm a bit ashamed to admit that I recorded it. Here it is, word for word, what he said.

I was in insurance, big company, lots of responsibility. I travelled a lot at the time, which is why, I suppose, my marriage flopped. Anyway, I was pretty much alone in everything when it happened.

It was like the *Titanic*. A whole stack of things had to go wrong at the same time for it to happen at all. First up we were three hours late taking off, which meant I missed my connecting flight and I would have to stay over for a night in this place, in a hotel paid for by the airline. Second, due to some complication with the booking, I didn't appear on the plane's manifest. I just didn't make the list they were using. Thirdly, I was dumb enough to give up my passport. The first two were not my fault, but the third was all down to me.

The airport here was already quite swish, the country was just beginning a big push for the tourist dollar at that time. I believe the new buildings were built with French money. Flash arrival hall and great carvings. It was very new then. I haven't seen it since.

We arrived at two in the morning. Very few staff were available and those that were, were not really on top of the job. I think it likely that the more senior people, who would have been more competent, were nicely tucked up in bed.

So, anyway, we were waiting there, a big crowd all surrounding a harried little chap who was handing out transfer and hotel vouchers. They were in no particular order, and he got in a bit of a mess. I waited for nearly an hour by which time everyone on the plane had a transfer except for me. Eventually there was just me and him standing there and he was empty-handed.

"What about me?" I asked him.

He looked at me with a semi-alarmed look on his face and said the fateful words: "Give me your passport and boarding pass and I'll go and check it out."

I was tired, I was too trusting, perhaps too eager not to show any prejudice against him. Whatever it was I handed over my documents and watched him disappear down a very long corridor and only after he was lost from view did I realise how foolish I'd been to hand over my only guarantee that I exist. It struck me immediately, if he did not return with my boarding pass and passport, how could I prove anything about myself or my flight?

He didn't come back. I'm not bitter about it. Who knows, in his position, maybe I would've done the same. He even looked a bit like me and was a similar age.

I waited for him to return, too nervous to sit down, pacing around a shiny corner of the arrival hall with its huge murals of

South Sea islands and liquor adverts. What was I to do? If I followed after him and he returned by a different path he wouldn't be able to find me. My spirits moved from unease to panic. Eventually, after a full hour, I walked down to the transfer check-in counters, which were all deserted. It was now four in the morning and, except for a few cleaners, the place was deserted.

There weren't many flights in those days; the massive airport buildings were something of a folly. It wasn't until nine the following morning that the desks were once again manned.

I know what you're thinking. "Why didn't you call someone?"

Well, that's all well and good and logical but you see it wasn't so easy in those days. There were no cellphones or even direct international dialling.

When I approached the transit desk that following morning, I could tell the young woman was a little afraid. She wasn't very experienced. When I explained my situation, her look of worry deepened.

"May I see your passport?" she said.

"One of your fellows took it," I answered.

At this she gave me a look that I felt I thoroughly deserved.

"I can tell you my name," I said pathetically. I couldn't even remember the flight number of the plane I was supposed to be flying out on that day.

She tapped away on her computer for what seemed like an age before calmly informing me that I did not exist.

Where my passport went, I still have no idea. Perhaps it was thrown onto the too-hard pile. I have no idea.

It was then that I noticed the young woman lift her gaze and look across to the man with an AK-47; the airport security were indistinguishable from regular army men. These guys seemed a bit miffed at not being able to shoot somebody. Their impassive expressions were very well rehearsed and convincing. I would much rather that these men not become involved, and so I moved away from the counter having smiled and thanked the transit clerk for her assistance and for being no help whatsoever.

What next? The first flights of the day took off. People streamed in and out. I decided to peek into the immigration hall where large groups were waiting to have their passports checked. These queues grew and grew through the day. There must have been a thousand people by lunch time. I drank some water and bought an energy bar from a vending machine that accepted a whole array of international coins.

This was about the point where my lack of faith in the life I had been living began to play its part. I could've, I suppose, gone back to the transit counter and made a fuss about my onward flight. I could've blustered and demanded. I suppose that would've done the trick, but I couldn't get out of my head something I had noticed earlier in the immigration hall. The flight crews were just waved through. Their uniform seemed to be enough. This was the time before 9/11, when security was less tight. All one needed was a little bag on wheels, which I already had, and a suitable jacket. The local airline stewards were made up of people from all over the world. I wouldn't look at all out of place. What if I walked out into this new world, free and fresh with everything open to me?

This was only a silly fantasy at that point but then fate, as she so often does, opened the door for me, so to speak.

On the back of one of those metal chairs that stand in rows all over air terminals was draped the maroon jacket of a chief steward, the owner of which was speaking in an animated manner to a downtrodden young stewardess who had upset him in some way.

It was then, that moment, that my life started spinning. I suppose I was more depressed, indeed crazier, than I had thought. I hadn't slept for more than a day. My heart felt reckless and desperate. Why not, for just once in my life, why not step into the unknown?

I casually swept up the jacket like it was the most natural

thing in the world. I went into the men's rest room and tried it on. It was a bit small but near enough. I emerged just as a flock of aircrew were sweeping through with that brisk manner they always have. I followed them past the immigration queues and into the special corridor reserved for them. I even managed a smile at the chap nodding us through.

I hadn't counted on a driver from this crew's transport company herding us onto his bus. It was just impossible not to get onto the bus without standing out from the crowd.

Everyone on the bus spoke French. At that time, I knew only a smattering of that language. It didn't seem to matter to them. They were all tired. They had been working for twelve hours at thirty-five thousand feet.

We arrived at the hotel and trooped like school children into the lobby and straight into the restaurant. This seemed to be the drill for the long-haulers. There were at least twenty in the crew; there must've been two flights arriving simultaneously. I sat down with them and ordered lunch with them. My shirt and trousers were not the same as theirs, and I didn't even have a tie, but these people were dead beat and no one took the slightest bit of interest in me or anything else, come to that. The food came and went in silence without incident but then a man appeared with a clipboard and one by one the aircrew rose to learn the number of their room. It was clear to me then that this was the point at which I had to give up this short-lived career as an air steward.

I wheeled my travel bag along the corridors looking for a rest room in which to change back into my own jacket. The resort hotel had a completely open-air feel. There weren't really any walls, just openings all around with outdoor restaurants, pools and, of course, the beach with the sea murmuring in the distance. I found the rest room and left my airline jacket behind.

I walked out of the hotel grounds to the yellow stucco arch that stood by the main road. It was at this point that the luxury of the resort came to an end and, looking both left and right, all that could be seen was a narrow, pot-holed stretch of tarmac.

I chose left. It was hot and twice taxis slowed and their eager-looking drivers looked at me expectantly. I decided to stay on foot. It was a strange business. When I look back on it, I cannot dismiss from the mind the idea that it was all fated. Never in my life have I had such a sensation of inevitability.

I had walked for no more than ten minutes when I found myself at the entrance to another beach hotel, but this one was very much more down-market. I turned into the narrow driveway. There was a short row of rooms with bamboo walls, concrete floors and plywood doors. There was a grass verge before the beach and a small children's playground with a couple of swings and a slide. The only other building on the premises was a covered space set with a few dining tables. One larger table served as a reception desk; there was a blanked-off corner that may have been an office and a kitchen area. The only person present was a woman standing behind a high bench that faced the beach. The noise of the wind and the surf meant that she was not aware of my arrival. I noticed that there was a small hotplate on the bench, and a sign advertising fresh pancakes. I walked down to the beach and turned to look at her.

It turned out that she was and still is the mistress of the businessman who owns the resort along the beach where I arrived with the airline crew, as well as this hotel. He has refurbished the rooms at this place and improved everything over the years but the woman selling the pancakes was the lady who checked you in and showed you to your room; she was the one who offered me this job. I have worked this little stretch of shoreline ever since.

THIS IS where I stopped the recording.

The hotel was still small but stylish and clearly successful. He didn't seem to do much. Indeed, I had seen what his 'work' consisted of. He spent a lot of his time giving massages to the guests at the hotel. He played quite a bit of volleyball with them too. I asked him, "Don't you get bored and miss your old life?"

"Bored? No. There are the paddle boats to look after and lots of sun lotion to apply. I'm fine."

And there I left it. For some reason it seemed quite wrong to say any more. I think it was the right decision, after all who was I to question this man's withdrawal from his former life?

Back in my room I took out the passport I had intended to return to him. This was the passport my father had used to enter New Zealand and to create a whole new life and identity for himself. This was the battered document my whole family was built on. I promised my father that I would find the real owner, make sure he was OK and return the passport to him. Dad always had it on his conscience.

I won't return the passport. I'll just tell Dad that I did and that the man in question is doing OK. That's enough.

THE MENTOR

1980

I MET my new trainee Jonathan and his wife Sue at the airport. It was, I believe, their first trip overseas. I had the picture on his application form so they couldn't have been easier to spot. They were young, innocent and beautiful. I introduced myself properly.

"Colin is my name. Lovely to meet you."

They were not used to formal greetings. They were common in their breeding and coarse in their manner. This notwithstanding their beauty. Theirs was the beauty of a wild stray lost in the thicket, not the beauty of thoroughbreds. Her warm, soft hand was folded awkwardly, as if she were touching a toad. His hand was too eager, like Tarzan grasping a ready vine. Their faces were clear and pale. They showed no sign of tiredness after the long flight. Smugness hung over them like mist over a forest on a damp morning. He was twenty-five, she not more than twenty-one.

I drove them to the hotel. They would not express their excitement. They upheld an absurd detachment trying to pretend that travelling eight thousand miles to a new, exotic world was an everyday occurrence for people of their type. They checked in, and I arranged to have a 'Welcome to Thailand' drink with them in the bar once they had taken their bags up.

"He looks dreadful," she said, not softly enough as they moved off to the lift.

I didn't catch his reply, but it was something containing the words 'old queer', which, as things turned out, was hardly prophetic.

In the bar, soft music was being played on one of those electronic gadgets and a Thai wench was crooning some ditty. When they appeared they had showered, but they obviously hadn't taken the opportunity to make love. They didn't have the wit to ride the wave of their new exotic setting. They were an odd combination of dullness and vitality.

We talked for a while of the business. Sue kept herself from me as if I were some sort of huge beetle. She was quite humourless. She was keeping herself solely for him. She would share nothing, not even a smile. Jon had the ready cynical humour that is so typical of cheap young men. It should have been funny, but it was a shade too cruel.

"You have come not a moment before time. There is so much work all at once. I have a couple of local men, but they won't take responsibility. You'll have to go it alone much of the time, but it's experience you would never get at home."

Before they left me that night, they leant forward right across the front of me and kissed. It was a long kiss in the grossest bad taste. I think it was that which sealed their fate.

I could not resist putting my hands behind their heads and squeezing them together. Sue pulled away as if hit by a stone. Jon, even though he didn't show it, was angry. But I was his boss and that class of person never loses sight of their venial motivation. A few moments after this, Sue vomited her rum and coke down the front of her dress. It could have endeared her to me except that her reaction was typically common. They left in a hurry.

"Come to dinner at the weekend," I called after them.

MY HOUSE WAS by the river. There was a balcony over the water. The thatched roof was very high and made from craggy native timbers which made it nearly always cool, such is the efficacy of the traditional design. I won't have a bar of air-conditioning. When I'm not there, my wife's family bathe in the river. Unfortunately, they never seem to catch anything lethal. Naturally, I won't have them in the house when I'm present. My wife had a cool, human discernment that fathomed my soul. She also had a slender lightness and a delicate grace that bewitched my senses. I called her Joy, but that was not her name. I can speak the language and could have easily called my wife by her correct name, but I choose not to. I think it would have been pretentious. To me she will always be Joy of the coffee shop at the Grace Hotel, gloriously attainable and open to my requirements. I never wanted her to dwindle into anything less. She was her beauty; it is not something that she owned as with Sue. How could an ancient, portly gentleman of my proclivities possibly resist such a treasure.

When they arrived at my home, Sue looked for all the world like a Barbie doll. She wore a patterned frock made for Marks and Spencer. Her long blonde hair and blue eyes were quite dazzling if you like that sort of plastic doll look. Joy welcomed her guest and honoured her with great humility and compassion. Jon was not a fool. He saw the contrast between them. My mission would be all too easily accomplished.

They ate far too much of the exquisite food my wife had prepared for them. That would change as they acclimatised to the heat. One can eat like that in cold climes only. They were already quite tanned; their light eyes were stunning against their pure bronzed European skin. Jon talked of football teams and his favourite shows on television. Sue spoke rarely and when she did her moral indignation was palpable. The situation was very clear in her mind, that is, as clear as anything could be in a mud-filled swamp of niceness. She gave nothing. Her meanness was her defining characteristic. I am proud to say that we never lost our dignity, which stood upon our duty to any guests in our house, no matter how crass they may be. This was not at all remarkable in Joy, for whom an air of poise is as natural as breathing. It was remarkable in me, however, as I am proud to claim that I have always been known for my intolerance.

We did have a company boat, the *Bella Donna*. A thirty-foot Impala. Not a real yacht, of course, with its detachable rudder and all that, but nevertheless she was a nippy thirty feet of fibreglass. Jonathan and Sue were in love with the idea of sailing, as most of the people in their class are. I took them out several times; Joy would never come as it made her seasick. On the first trip there was quite a blow on. These modern boats are like saucers. You can't get a sense of the wind when a yacht refuses to heel. It seems like nothing is happening and then suddenly you go over. Not that we did capsize but that's how it felt. There we were, making hull speed in the Gulf of Siam and I let the boy have his first steer. The boat wasn't handling well, and he had to hang on for grim death just to keep her on course. Once or twice we almost broached. I liked scaring them. Call it revenge if you like. After all, no one ever called me beautiful.

It was during the first trip that I decided I would have that plump little body that Sue guarded so jealously. It might surprise you but that had not occurred to me before. You see, in thirty years I had grown used to much finer meat. However, when I saw the tough little waist and ample breasts barely contained within the bikini, I decided that it might be diverting; like a Christmas lunch in a working-class household.

Jon learned quickly how to manage the boat. On the second trip, he produced a book which he reckoned had some ideas about how we could make the boat handle better. It basically boiled down to easing the main sheet, and do you know, it worked.

He was one of the very few of the masses who genuinely deserved to be promoted from the ranks. He was deft and steady with his work on the foredeck and a natural helmsman. Sue was very good in the galley and, despite that first night, never chundered at sea, even in a blow. She tidied constantly and only occasionally got in the way. Had she been mute one might have enjoyed having her on board. As it was, the whine of her inanities was a test of one's patience. Jon endured it, as men of his meagre experience do. The second afternoon we were caught in a channel with a fishing boat coming straight towards us. We were going to windward and a carefully timed tacking manoeuvre was required if we were to avoid both the rocks and the fisherman. Jon timed the moment to go about to perfection.

The boy impressed me with his work too. He would make a man once I had knocked the decency out of him. The lad had never lived and never would when tied to a woman like that. Such females may be good for something in the class they are born into but just what that is I cannot say.

Each evening we worked late, sometimes into the next day. I knew I had surprised him. I have always had stamina and mental endurance. It comes from choosing a profession well within my capabilities. I have always felt myself to be working at about ten per cent of my capacity. He thought I would be out of date. He didn't know that part of being grown up means being able to concentrate on what you're doing. I could feel him beginning to admire me. As he had no philosophy of his own, mine was bound to impress him. Very often I have a liberating effect on young men. Few men can make a life for themselves, but many can acquire maturity if properly brought on.

About nine one evening, when I decided that he was ready, I suggested meeting at the Koko bar. "Just a drink" was how I had put it. The bar scene in Thailand is very well documented. I need not fill in the details. You can get a drink at the Koko, but really it's a knocking shop. Young Thai lasses of all description sit behind a glass enclosure twittering like birds. You can see them, but they cannot see you. It's a kind of heaven. Jon was an ordinary young man and there was nothing particularly fine about him. Given the way people grow up nowadays, with no idea of themselves or of the traditions that have made the world, my task of corrupting him could not have been easier. Jon was not a man capable of love, you see. Few people are. Naturally I chose a woman from behind the screen. I left him to wait for me.

Naturally, less than a week later, he went again, only this time by himself. Soon it was four or five times a week. I would imagine that Sue was aware that first night. Within a couple of weeks Jon was staying at my house. Sue was by herself. It was obvious what she would do. She thought she could make him jealous. All I had to do was knock on the door. She would have slept with a dog in order to get back at her husband.

It was not a success. She was like an automaton. I didn't enjoy it. But it had been a perfectly executed plan and Jon could hardly complain at me. Instead he fell back on that curious nonsense about he and Sue "doing their own thing".

I was soon able to introduce her to a young stockbroker and that did the trick. She followed this with a two-week holiday in Hawaii with a Chinese businessman. That got her into a very expensive set, well out of my league. She'll be a millionaire by now if I read her right. Meanness has its compensations, and one could read avarice in Sue at five hundred yards.

Had they stayed in Middle Wallop or wherever it was, they would probably have gone on forever. As it was, Sue became a high-class professional. They say she has learned to dress with great taste and has developed an interest in Eastern spirituality.

And Jon?

Well, Jon now lives in Singapore. He's a marketing manager for a company that manufactures personal computers. His new wife is quite lovely. He takes the trouble to pronounce her name properly. They say she rules him with a rod of iron.

I dare say Joy would do that to me if I let her. Rest assured, I won't let her.

THE HIT

The drone hovered very low right above my head. I've heard they have cameras in them. As the thing began to lower the package, I made it as clear as I could that there was no way it could have been meant for me. I waved my hands and made every gesture I could think of but still the thing came down and unlatched itself on my lawn. The small box lay watching me as the squealing flying machine angled its way back into the sky.

The impertinence of the whole event made me angry. I mean, goodness gracious. The few people who know me, know that I am Hindu and that I loathe Christmas presents even more than I loathe Christmas itself. No one would have been at all interested in sending me a gift. I didn't even remotely desire a gift. Indeed, any contact with anyone is something I am required to control.

The shattering of my tranquil little universe was so complete. The perfect picture ruined. The sun had been already quite low and was inundating my garden with a delicious yellow light. I was watching the sea in the distance from my patio, taking a break from the *Bhagavata Purana*, the book of God that I read at this time every year, thinking how well I had done avoiding the whole dreary business of Christmas. It was almost time for aam panna; nothing was more cooling and refreshing than this beverage made from mango juice and mint. Soon I would begin cooking my evening meal while listening to Asha Bhosle. Peace was everywhere, just as I wanted it to be.

It had not been difficult to avoid this most ugly of holidays. All one had to do was avoid people and any broadcast media and switch off one's phone. My house on the cliff, despite being one of a row, does not afford a view of anyone else's windows or gardens and so I hadn't seen as much as a blinking fairy light. And now I was forced to deal with this wretched aerial invasion.

I carried the box into my kitchen and sliced through the thick masking tape with a carving knife. The box contained just two items: a small, beautifully designed revolver which was loaded and ready to go, and a close-up photograph of my next-door neighbour.

I knew him instantly, not just because of our stunted conversations while taking out the garbage bins but also because the young man was a successful show business figure. He was, I believe, an actor or a TV presenter or something along those lines. He was a very good-looking young character.

Now I have read my fair share of thrillers and seen dozens of films where hit men are set up just the way that I seemed to have been. But I'm not a hit man. I used to work in the finance office for the council in Palmerston North. This was the first time I had held a gun in my life. It was, however, quite clear to me what was going on.

You see, I am number 11. That's the whole thing in a nutshell. The young chap who was to be rubbed out (I'm afraid that term may be a little dated, but I don't know a more modern one), he lives at number 13. The numbers go 7, 9, 13, 11, then 15. It was all to do with how the original farmland was subdivided. Anyway, I had seen the fellow who had just moved into number 9 and if ever I saw an assassin, it was him. He just had that look about him. Eyes very close together, foreign accent, you know the type of thing.

So. What was I to do? Well, it's not as obvious as you might think. Clearly a ring to the local police station was called for. This would have indeed been the very thing, but there was a difficulty with that. I myself was wanted by them. You see, my seaside hideaway, of which I am so proud, was purchased with funds embezzled from the good people of Palmerston North, and while they may be good, they are not a forgiving people.

I had no time left for any further deliberation. My doorbell made its shrill call, demanding attention. I peeped around the corner into the hall and through the window I saw the sinister gentleman from number 9. He must have seen the drone and the package descending. Well, you might say, why not give him the gun and be shot of the whole business. Oh dear, *shot*. I didn't mean to use that term. No, that was not an option. I was hardly about to abet such a crime. Ah, you might say, surely you are jumping to conclusions; but think about it, what else could a revolver and a picture mean? I hope you see my point.

So I refrained from opening the door and ran out into my garden. I must warn my neighbour, that was the thing, I must tell him to 'take a powder', which I believe is the correct term in a situation such as this, in the moving picture world the phrase is very common.

I attempted to get over the garden wall. It was reasonably easy on my side but on the other it was overgrown with rambling rose bushes. The whole garden was a blaze of flowers; the sea of roses that I was grappling with were only bit players. I was able to take this in despite being hopelessly entangled in the thorns.

It was then I heard the voice.

"Brent, there's an Indian fella stuck in your roses."

Only moments later Brent the movie star and his girlfriend were looking up at me. One of the reasons I'd been having such difficulty in getting over the wall was that in my anxiety I was still clinging on to Brent's picture in my right hand. Brent must have seen this, for he said, "Jesus, mate, if you want the photo signed you only have to knock on the door."

"No," I answered, "no, there's going to be a hit."

At this, Brent smiled bashfully. "All my films are hits, mate, no trouble there."

"Oh God," I answered. "If you help me down, I'll explain."

"You're making a real mess of my roses, mate."

Brent seemed to be quite annoyed by this, but he forged a path through the flowers and lifted me onto the ground. He towered over me, a good six feet, I would guess.

"Look," I began, pulling the revolver out of my pocket.

"Hold on there, fella," said Brent, showing me both of his palms and gallantly stepping in front of his girlfriend.

"No," I answered, "these came down from the sky."

"What?" Now he was sure I was bonkers, and his face showed panic.

"No." I tried to sound reassuring. "No, a drone, your picture and the gun, they were delivered to me by drone. I think they came to the wrong person, but whoever should have received them …"

It was at that point that Brent made his move. He snatched the gun away from me in a flash. I mean quite literally in a flash, the gun went off, doing even more damage to the roses.

The sound of the loud bang was very bad news. For surely the man at number 9 would have heard.

"Oh dear," I exclaimed, somewhat inadequately.

I think this gentle exclamation may have worked in my favour; I mean I think it likely that ruthless hitmen probably express themselves somewhat more forcefully.

Brent looked at me with a look of puzzlement on his face. He said, almost as much to himself as to me, "No one wants to kill me. You must have it wrong, mate."

"OK," I answered, glad that he seemed to be concluding that I wasn't the villain in this drama. "But why were these things dropped onto my lawn, and why is there a very shady character knocking on my door? He's an assassin, I'm sure."

This turned into a rhetorical question because before Brent could attempt an explanation, his doorbell rang. It was one of those loud clanging ones that would have been perfect on a castle drawbridge in the Middle Ages. It seemed to me the very voice of doom.

"Don't answer it," I whispered.

"You go, Cherry," said Brent to his girlfriend, somewhat to my surprise.

"Not on your life," Cherry answered, which seemed to me the perfect reply.

"No one wants to do me in." Brent was again talking to himself. "I mean," he went on, "I do romantic comedies. I know they're not everyone's cup of tea but that's hardly my fault."

It was then we heard the garden gate burst open.

The man from number 9 literally fell into the garden. He'd charged the gate and his momentum sent him flying onto the lawn. He ended up lying at Brent's feet.

"Who the hell are …"

Brent still had the gun in his hand, and this was probably why he wasn't allowed to finish the sentence. The fellow on the floor did some weird kind of gymnastics and before you could say Jack Robinson, he held the gun and Brent was on the floor.

"This belongs to me," said number 9. He clearly felt embarrassed by the loss of the weapon in the first place, but he quickly regained his dignity.

"What's this about?" asked Cherry.

"I'm a bodyguard," answered number 9. "I've been assigned to look after Brent. Don't think we haven't checked you out, young lady,' he said, looking at Cherry. "We know you're not who you say are. People like you are dangerous."

It seemed to me that if anyone was dangerous it was him — leaving guns about, bashing down gates and knocking over film stars.

"I wasn't told any of this, and anyway I don't need a bodyguard." Brent said this while getting to his feet. He was looking at Cherry questioningly.

"You'll need me soon enough, believe me," said number 9. At last he slipped on the safety catch and put the gun in his belt.

I was most impressed with this. It was an automatic action just as one sees in the movies although I never understand why they use the belt and not their pocket.

Number 9 continued. It was clear that a certain dignity had returned to his ample frame. "Bodyguards are most effective when they're hidden. By living next door, I could watch you and, more importantly, I can see anyone coming after you before they see me."

"So who are you then?" said Brent to Cherry.

"Nobody. That's the problem. I'm Raelene from Palmerston North, if you must know."

Oh no, I thought, *not there*.

"You can't blame me for wanting to sound a bit more exotic."

"There is nothing exotic about being a refugee from Siberia," said number 9.

"There is if you come from Palmerston North," said Cherry.

Brent turned his attention to number 9.

"But who said I needed a bodyguard and why do I need one?"

"Let's just say you're in the running, a very high-profile part. You've become a valuable property."

"Wow," exclaimed Brent, "high-profile, really."

This information clearly swamped everything else. Silence settled over us as Brent absorbed his good news. I felt I should take my leave of them.

"I think I should go now," I began. "I'm very sorry for the misunderstanding and about the roses."

"No," said Brent. "No, mate, no. Remember it's Christmas, I

can throw another couple of steaks on the barbie. We can have a few drinks."

Oh my God, I thought. *Christmas, no matter how fast I run it catches up with me.*

It would seem so impolite to refuse such a gracious invitation after invading their garden in such a ridiculous manner. There was nothing else to do but accept.

"No steaks," I said, "but if you have anything vegetarian. And …"

"Yes?" said Brent.

"Perhaps you could sign your photograph."

AT LEAST IT WAS A JOB

AT LEAST IT WAS A JOB. It was a meagre salary. No prospects, but it was money coming in. Alice had a BA and was quite intelligent in a vague kind of way, but it had been eleven months since she graduated, and this opening was only her second interview.

Customers rang with their complaints. All you had to do was follow the procedure laid out by each company. It was like a complaints call centre, only the punters were never to be told that they were not dealing directly with the company concerned.

On her first day, for the first forty-five minutes, the phone had not rung. Also in the office was her only colleague. She had received no more than a nod on entering the room. A strange character, this colleague. Beautifully dressed and generally turned out. He was reading a novel in German. It would have been natural to speak. But he hadn't said a word. There was just the nod and a cursory glance.

Still the phone did not ring.
"Is it always this quiet?"
"No."
"I'm Alice Quinn."
"Mark Bryant."

"Do you always dress so smartly?"

"I suppose so. It's a habit and anyway these are the only kind of clothes that I possess."

"Makes me feel really scruffy."

"Can't help that."

Mark put down his novel.

"This is my first job, I'm quite nervous really."

"You'll soon get used to it. Sometimes they shout a bit, but it's only words. The important thing is to not shout back. The calmer you are, the better. Nothing to it really."

"They never gave me any training, just these forms to read. I'm sure I'll make a mess of it."

"I don't believe you will. They'll hear how young you are and that will make most of them more placid."

Then it began; it was like someone had thrown a switch. From nine on the dot the phone never stopped for six hours straight. Alice coped well enough. The forms were filled in, the complaints logged. By the end of the first hour the routine had become boring. At the end of the first week the work had become extremely tedious. Alice coped. It was a job and she stuck to it for two years.

Often afterwards Alice wondered what would have happened had there been no accident. Would she have ever learned anything more about Mark Bryant?

She had always felt in control of her little Suzuki. But the old lady who had been walking sprightly enough down the footpath suddenly veered into the road. There was nothing Alice could do. By the time the ambulance had left, the car towed and the police dealt with, it was twelve o'clock. She went in to work anyway. She hoped to take her mind off it, but the police had measured the skid marks. What was her speed? She knew it was sixty or seventy, well over the maximum.

For the first hour at work she had been fine, but suddenly she found she was crying. She kept sobbing.

"That poor woman. It's all my fault."

She would've been so much more grateful to Mark as he sought to calm her if only he had not maintained exactly the manner he used on the phone with the callers.

He was infinitely calm and logical but cold and formal. He seemed totally unaffected by emotion, be it his own or anyone else's.

It transpired that the elderly lady was a dementia sufferer, who had inadvertently wandered out of her nursing home. Her injuries were slight with no broken bones. There was, however, the issue of Alice's speed and charges were laid. Mark casually suggested a friend of his to represent her.

"I did practise law for a while, I know my way around the system." He smiled, which was a very rare event.

And so she was represented at the trial. Mark organised it that there was no payment. The case went exactly as he had predicted. There was no denying that she had been speeding and it was no use claiming that the eighty-nine-year-old woman had leapt out in front of her. She was found guilty, heavily fined and disqualified from driving for six months.

Mark had observed the proceedings in court dressed much the same as he always was. His manner was professional. He was very helpful, no one could have done better. By then Alice had resigned the job. She couldn't bear the tedium any longer.

After the trial, standing in the bitter wind outside the district court, she and her mother invited Mark to lunch. He had refused. Had to get back to work apparently. As though it really mattered. He walked away from them with the briefest of nods and the tiniest smile.

"He's like a machine," observed Alice's mother. "Like an alien out of *Dr Who*."

"You should be more grateful, Mum, he really helped. He's never asked for anything in return. He's incredibly patient."

"Oh, I'm grateful, but he's like a zombie."

And then, out clubbing one evening, Alice met Sean who was soon her husband, next she had three kids and after that her mother died. All through she felt that life was happening to her. All she had to do was go along with events. Her children did well at school and soon her daughters were looking for a job. In the twenty-five years that had passed it had become even harder for those with a BA. There was nothing out there.

One evening, only too typically, Sean came home with one of his extravagant purchases. A sixty-two-inch LED television. Alice had long ago given up trying to stop him; he earned well enough, but they had nothing saved. Even before having his evening meal he was drilling the wall and fixing the bracket. With great pride he fitted the huge television into the slots and stepped back to observe how fine it looked and how much space they had saved.

What happened next would have been funny had the machine not cost over four thousand dollars. There was a barely discernible click as a weld gave way. And the set crashed to the floor. It was undamaged except for a scratch across the soft pliable screen. Sean suspected the thing hadn't been welded at all; there was just a coat of paint holding it together. On the receipt from the electronics warehouse there was a number to call if the purchaser was not completely satisfied.

"Call them," said Sean, leaving the dirty work to Alice. "Give them a piece of your mind."

The voice was unmistakable. Even after twenty years, there was no one else who had that cool, precise manner.

"Mark, Mark Bryant? It is you, isn't it?"

"Yes, how can I help you?"

"It's Alice, Alice Quinn that was. Remember?"

"Alice, yes, of course I remember, what is your problem?"

"How are you?"

"I'm about the same, somewhat older."

During the pause that followed, Alice wondered if it was worth persisting. There was a stubbornness in her that couldn't allow such iciness to win. It was inhuman. This was the reason why she overcompensated.

"We must meet up sometime for a coffee."

"I don't actually drink coffee. What exactly is the problem?"

There was no breaking down the doors. Alice told him what had happened and answered all the questions as he quizzed her about part numbers and dates of purchase.

At the end there was merely a pause before he said, "Is that all I can help you with?"

Alice was overcome by an unexpected passion.

"For God's sake, Mark, we worked side by side for two years and you were a great friend to me in times of trouble, surely you can be … civil."

Alice had never used the word before, but she found herself using Mark's language. There was another pause, quite a long one this time.

"I'm sorry," he said finally, "but you know what I'm like. I'd like to have a drink with you, just name the time and place."

Alice now realised that she hadn't actually meant it. A coffee 'sometime' actually means sometime never. But of course she was trapped.

"Barnetts tomorrow night, five-thirty. We can catch up."

"Yes, we can … catch up."

"Why did I do that?" whispered Alice as she put the phone down.

He was not much changed, heavier perhaps, balder but then he had never had much hair. He was waiting for her and stood up formally as she arrived. As they shook hands, he deliberately averted his eyes. She had always sensed his fear of people. She had made a special effort to look smart, and she was glad she had, for Mark was as immaculate as ever.

"I was amazed to find you still in the same job."

"Oh, it's very different now, we enter the complaints directly onto a computer, and there are eight of us running a twenty-four-hour service. There are rumours about closing us down and exporting the jobs to the Philippines, but I don't know if anything will come of it."

She waited for him to ask how she was doing but he didn't. He just gazed at her strangely. It made her nervous and she found herself gabbling on, giving a potted history of her life and her kids. Mark looked totally uninterested, bored even. At this a silence developed. To fill it, Alice found she could not resist plunging into a question that had baffled her over the years.

"What I'd really like to know, Mark, is why you haven't done more. In your job, I mean. You're obviously a very smart man."

"I used to be a judge, one of the youngest in the country."

"So what happened?"

He looked at her, but his eyes seemed to glaze in puzzlement.

"It's hard to explain. You might say corruption or perhaps lack of insight."

He seemed prepared to leave it there, but Alice could not.

"What do you mean?"

He paused and put his knuckles to his lips as though ordering things in his mind.

"Alice, you must not think that I ever forgot about you. To tell the truth I was really taken with you. But you were twenty years younger than me and I ... well, I didn't have much to offer. In truth, Alice, there's hardly been a day gone by without my thinking about your lovely fresh face ... Sorry."

Oh God, thought Alice. She could think of no way of replying.

"You ask why I haven't done more. Well, the problem was, indeed is, that when one works in the law one is part of a system that so distorts things ... corrupts things ..." He tailed off into silence but Alice could tell he wanted to explain further. He looked up at her; she could see he was trying to be even-handed and reasonable and to avoid emotion.

"There is a safety net of course. The rules, the law as written should be unambiguous. Some people can survive. For a long while I could. I was a district court judge for eight years. I don't think I caused more suffering than your average judge."

At this point the coffee arrived and this seemed to lighten his mood.

"It wasn't just one case. For years I had felt my judgement inadequate. I would always try to serve the interest of the people who relied upon me, but over and over again I felt I had let them down.

"Well," said Alice, "you did what you thought was right. That's something." She smiled inadequately in her desperation to be gone. "And now, well, at least it's a job."

"Yes," he answered, realising at last how separate they were and how little Alice resembled what he imagined her to be.

"Bye then, see you again sometime," Alice said, rising from her chair.

"Whenever you have a complaint to make, I suppose."

He managed a smile as she left. She had to get the takeaways for dinner.

He felt wounded, there was a rent in his heart. It was sharply painful.

He paid with a note. This left the right change for his bus fare.

TALENT AND CONFIDENCE

"Talent and confidence — that's what it takes. Just one or the other isn't enough, but if you have both you'll be successful."

Oh no, I thought, *Barry is going to hold forth.*

He had an uncanny instinct to say the wrong thing at the wrong time and this was very much not the moment to be putting the world to rights.

It was the Christmas staff party. Every year they made us go to this barn of a restaurant to sit for hours among hundreds of other worker bees and wait for the tepid mass-produced junk food to arrive. Then there would be the speeches, which seemed to have been flown in directly from cuckoo land, so optimistic and positive they were, totally ignoring how much injustice and exploitation was going on.

To show how democratic the company was, the directors would be sprinkled among us. One could see that the bosses hated this event as much as we did, but the big guns insisted on turning up year after year, and this year we had struck the jackpot. Bill Keane himself, the founder and managing director, was sitting right beside me with Barry across the table from us. Keane was still only thirty-five; starting from nothing he had become a millionaire by the time he was twenty. The business papers said he was heading towards a billion.

All of this made no difference to Barry. He was sure to go on as if he had the whole world sorted, fully understood and explained. He is very smart, don't get me wrong. He reads a lot, books that is, not just websites, and he was a good programmer, but he was missing the social awareness gene, that little voice that should have been whispering in his ear: "Not now, Barry, now is the time to be careful." Bill Keane could close our section down on a whim and programming jobs were not easy to find at our advanced age. We were both pushing thirty.

"You see," Barry went on, "you must have talent at something, otherwise what are you going to give to the world? And you have to have confidence, otherwise you can never make your voice heard, no matter how great the things you have to say."

Barry looked across the table at Keane. This was new; obviously Barry was at least aware of Keane and perhaps even interested in what his response would be. I have never seen him stop for anyone else in all the years I have known him. Keane seemed not to be listening. He hadn't said a word to anyone since arriving. There had been a slight tightening of his lips as he sat down on the uncomfortable wooden bench. That may have been a smile in our direction, but I can't be sure.

Well, Barry was never one to be put off by a lack of reaction. He was sure to dig deeper.

"Some people might say you have to be lucky and that you can't get anywhere without a few good breaks, and some might say that persistence is the key, that is, never giving up, but you see the point is that if you have talent then the gift itself will push you on, no matter how unlucky you are. The talent will make you persistent. It's like having another being living inside you, and as long as you have the confidence to go out into the world and make your own mark, well then, there's nothing you can't achieve."

I could feel that Keane was getting more and more uncomfortable. I had read articles about him. Apparently as a child he had suffered from ADHD. I'm not sure that's a condition that ever goes away. His attention was certainly wandering around the room. It was uncanny how he scanned every other table but showed no interest in the things close to him, and he was certainly hyperactive; his thigh was juddering up and down in a throbbing rhythm that had nothing to do with the awful Muzak that was playing.

Keane had been messily divorced three times from a selection of supermodels that he had abused in various ways. I suppose that in that respect at least there's evidence of an attention disorder, but I don't believe in the labelling of personality disorders. The labels are surely too sweeping. It seems to me that all personalities are disordered and inevitably disordered in their own peculiar way. We were a group of programmers, for example, and we certainly had plenty of the expected semi-autistic traits, but we were hardly similar people. It seems to me autistic to want to have a catch-all phrase that enables you to say "I can explain this person with one condition." Take Barry, for example, he's a well-adjusted guy. He understands things pretty well. He has a wife and a little girl, and he seems to get along fine despite the hours he has to work, but he does have this thing, this desire to come up with theories and push them out into the world.

Anyway, he and everyone else were doing their best to keep up some sort of pleasant conversation. Everyone, that is, except the star of the show, Bill Keane, who remained obdurately silent and detached. I have to say, I thought it mean of him. It was a big deal for us to have him there. Surely he could have at least smiled and pretended to enjoy himself.

Finally, the food turned up, cold, as predicted, and also kind of random. Everyone was either missing something or had too much of something. Keane didn't eat a thing. His plates came and went completely undisturbed. He did drink the table water, seemingly gallons of it. I had a couple beers and ate everything put in front of me. The company was not into perks. We had to account for every moment of our time. May as well get what I could out of them.

Next came the speeches. As usual they were excruciating. Apparently we were all 'fantastic'. This word was used nine times. We knew it would be popular; we even had a bet on how many times it would occur. Barry had made the highest prediction, so he won the money. We had all made covert triumphant expressions as our number was reached only to inwardly groan as our figure was surpassed. We would have been much more demonstrative had our superstar boss not been among us. In truth the word could hardly have been more inappropriate. There was nothing even remotely resembling a fantasy in anything we had done during the year; it had been a hard slog with a real struggle going on just to keep our edge and maintain our place in the market. Our business could implode at any time. There was always this trembling thought at the back of everyone's mind. Another source of disquiet was the Quixotic personality of Keane. He had been known to take extreme risks and to make ill-considered decisions. No one ever knew what he would do next and he wasn't telling anyone. Indeed, even when asked to propose a toast he just shook his head. The head of sales, who was running our celebration, seemed knocked back by this, embarrassed even. One felt a tension there between the two men.

Once the speeches were over and the tepid Christmas pudding served up, Keane was gone. In a moment, he pushed his chair back and pretty much ran out of the room. It would have been so much better had he not turned up at all. Everyone noticed, and I'm sure they all felt slighted. He was on the news constantly as a bona fide celebrity. Of course there was no duty imposed upon him to be open with us, but it would have been so easy for him to pretend to us that we were worth talking to. He didn't have to tell us his plans, but it would have cost him nothing to spread a little of his stardust about the table.

People were sure to ask me what he talked about. That was not going to be much of a conversation.

Naturally, once he'd gone everyone relaxed. Around our table there was almost a chorus of the same exclamation; not said out loud, it hung in the air for a few seconds until Barry, the most fearless among us, gave it voice. "What a dick," he said, to everyone's great relief.

But I'm sure in all of our minds lingered a sense of disappointment. For Keane was paying our salaries every week and surely there must be something to the man, something that made him stand out.

The following week the online newsletter ran pictures of the celebration. There were several of Keane, which had been crudely Photoshopped, giving the impression that he had joined in with everything. There was one showing him raising his glass to the camera, which was clearly from a completely different event.

We could only smile at how fake the all-inclusive corporate structure was. Keane often boasted in print about how we were all equal parts of a team. The strange thing was that this man had achieved so much; surely, I thought, there had to be something to him. He must have some quality to account for his stellar career.

The question nagged at me. I expect there was some personal resentment or even anger swirling about in me that pressed me to find out more. So it was that I went digging. All the stuff online and all the biographies, the favourable ones and the attacks, I read the lot.

The picture that emerged came down to single-mindedness, a cool determination to win, to be into things early and to push them along with enormous energy. It was some time before I realised that there was no idea. No central skill set. No breakthrough. There was not a single moment when he had made a great move. It seemed to come down to ensuring that he was in the right place and taking over companies with original ideas at just the right time.

Then something happened that made it all clear. Something that was common to everything Bill Keane had done.

The desire to share my discovery was overwhelming. It was a Saturday and there was no way I was going to wait until Monday to show what I had found to Barry, after all, he was directly involved.

I knocked on the door of his apartment. Barry's wife, Julie, answered. She was the kind of person that anyone would want for a partner in life. The quality she had that made her so great was how calm she was. She seemed to find it so easy just to take life as it comes and watch quietly as it slid by, while always bringing to it a delicious sense of fun. It seemed to me that Barry was a very lucky man. She invited me into their home; a tableau was set out on their living room floor. Barry had built up an array of boxes and drawings and toys which represented a farmyard with all kinds of buildings and animals set about, and in the middle was his three-year-old daughter pulling a tractor. She was going to the market, which was a large brown paper bag with windows and advertising signs drawn on it with crayons.

When Barry stood up to greet me, the little girl hardly noticed, so deeply was she engaged in her world.

"So," he said, "what's up?" He was clearly surprised to see me there.

"I've got something to show you. It explains everything about Keane. This makes it plain, it's all so simple."

Barry's expression showed puzzlement and not a little displeasure.

"Why do you care about that dick?"

"Look," I said, ignoring his question. I opened the company magazine I'd been holding under my arm. There on a double-page spread was a picture of Keane alongside an article which he had written. The article was entitled 'The Secret of Success'.

The first line read: "Talent and confidence — that's what it takes. Just one or the other is not enough, but if you have both you'll be successful."

I looked at Barry in triumph.

"It's exactly, word for word what you said at the Christmas party. This is what Keane does, he just steals other people's ideas. It all fits together now. That's his talent."

Barry was as frank as always. "That's not a talent and Bill Keane is not a successful man. You need to think about your own life, not how he operates." His attention was already slipping back to his child, who was tottering towards him across the carpet.

THE LAKE POETS

It was summer but the day was cold and the clouds heavy with rain. The lake shone black and the hills beyond were devoid of all colour. Ratby gazed out upon the scene from the window of his room in the boarding house where he stayed during the season. He was enraptured.

"Earth has not anything to show more fair," he quoted aloud, and he meant it. He loved the bleakness of the lakes just as Wordsworth had. He loved the rain that was falling steadily and the shadowed hills. The whole point of the Romantics was the feeling reflected inward, not the outward view. Coleridge said as much many times. The beauty of a bright summer's day misses the point altogether. He wondered whether any of his charges this day would understand that this was the perfect weather in which to see the home of the great men. Sometimes they did. Not often, but sometimes.

Ratby held his smile; it was a challenge offered to the assembling tour group. There were twelve today. They had travelled by train from London. This was considered more authentic, more appropriate; and it was true that most of the Lake poets had lived on into the age of steam.

"Ladies and gentlemen, welcome to Windermere."

They kept a stock of umbrellas and as Ratby handed them out, he smiled at each of his customers, reading their lives in their faces.

"Now you must tell me where you are all from."

He had found that the thing that pleased tourists the most was to talk about themselves. If he could get them talking among themselves about themselves, his job was made a great deal easier.

To Ratby's dismay it turned out that all twelve of them were from the same college in Lincoln, Nebraska and that they all carried notebooks. This meant they all desired facts. Ratby had very few of these. His only real qualification was that he loved poetry and could recite reams of it. That is what had got him the job. There was precious little else that he was qualified to do. A further discouraging fact about the assembled group was that their teacher was with them. The man introduced himself as Robert A. Torncast, Doctor of Literature. Ratby felt sure that the qualification was given not as boast but instead as a way of establishing a rapport with a fellow scholar. Ratby merely felt intimidated. All he could hope for was that the good doctor would take over the tour and do his job for him. It did not happen. All twelve merely waited politely expecting Ratby to enlighten them.

Ratby had been caught like this several times before. Perhaps the worst case was when a young Canadian had asked him: "What really happened that morning of December the fourth, seventeen ninety-seven?"

Ratby knew it was no good trying to wing it, they always found him out. His only option was to fall back on the poems themselves and what they convey. This was his home ground.

"I want you to reflect upon why it is that you are here today. Is it the beauty of the landscape? The weather? Is it because you are going to see some famous performance? No, of course it is none of these things. No, it is because of the love two young men held for life itself. For them, 'Bliss was it in that dawn to be alive, but to be young was very heaven'. How to express this love? They were both bright, educated young men well versed in the Classics. Both had the gift of verse, obviously they would turn to poetry. But what was poetry in 1770 when Wordsworth was born?" (This was the one date Ratby could remember. He looked about him proudly as all twelve of them wrote it down.) "Poetry then was a formal exercise in learning. It had to be filled with illusions which only people of high learning could grasp, it had to conform to strict meter and remain within the tight constraints of classical form. It had nothing to do with the fire burning in the hearts of these two young men. What was needed and what they gloriously provided was a *revolution*."

Ratby paused for dramatic effect.

"A revolution of the type that had happened first in your own proud land and then in France. A revolution of the type that Beethoven, born the same year as Wordsworth, that's 1770, had provided in music. Rather than merely travelling over the well-worn path followed by their predecessors, these two young men struck out in a new direction. They travelled inwards into their own hearts and gave form to what they found there. This is what we mean by Romanticism. Wordsworth and Coleridge paved the way for Byron and Keats and the rest, just as surely as George Washington made possible Abraham Lincoln."

The trick was to appear passionate. As long as you appear passionate, Ratby found that no one cared whether you knew anything or not. It was all working a treat. It was purely fortuitous that these people hailed from a place named after the great American President. Not that Ratby would admit that it was.

"We have not yet touched on their particular genius, one which I am sure that they discovered together, although Coleridge was always the more original of the two. The genius of the Lake poets relies on the delineation of the way in which nature affects the human heart. To take the most famous poem and the most famously misunderstood poem of all; I mean of course 'Daffodils'. This poem is not about the yellow flowers that crowd the hills here in the spring. It is a poem about the perception of beauty and the effect it has upon the soul. Tintern Abbey is …"

Ratby saw to his dismay that he was losing his audience. Rain was dripping off the noses of the young girls who were trying to appear interested, but they clearly were having trouble enduring Ratby's oration. Two boys were fighting with the umbrellas. It didn't matter, he had proven himself passionate, he had performed his role adequately.

"Well, enough of my chatter, let's walk to the house, shall we? The house they lived in for … many years. This way."

The house was, in its way, a splendid example of its time. Small, cold, dark, creaky and full of original artifacts and even a few precious manuscripts. Ratby didn't know quite what to make of something he heard Torncast say to one of the students.

"Wordsworth was John Lennon, introspective, edgy and basically an egotist. Coleridge was Paul McCartney, a storyteller and a fine craftsman. I'll lend you a paper I've written on the comparison."

Ye gods, thought Ratby.

The tour groups were always given lunch at the Stolen Goose pub. The building went back way beyond 1800, but it had been gutted so many times it was extremely unlikely that either of the Lake poets would have recognised it.

Much to his chagrin, Ratby was not included in the lunch party, unless someone in the party was kind enough to invite him and pay for him. As the groups had already paid out quite a sum, few were willing to do this.

Torncast quickly grasped the situation and proved himself a generous man.

"What's your favourite poem?" asked a girl who clearly had

no interest in his answer. Several of them turned to Ratby seemingly expecting him to hold forth.

"You must understand that your question is like comparing one feeling with another. Each is individual, and it all depends on one's mood and especially how mature one has become emotionally. Many people return to the poems of their youth in old age and see nothing in them or see them as something entirely different."

"But which is your favourite poem?"

"'The Prelude'," answered Ratby, hoping to shut her up. To his amazement the girl began to recite some of the poem's most obscure stanzas. The recitation was excruciating, utterly devoid of humanity.

"Tracy has a photographic memory," put in Torncast. "She is a phenomenon."

"I know five hundred books by heart," said Tracy. "I'm a savant."

"It must be wonderful to be able to remember so many facts," said Ratby, feeling pathetic.

He was on his third glass of wine. He was not a heavy drinker usually; he knew how vulnerable a man in his position was to falling under the grip of alcohol, but there was something about the day that made him accept when Torncast offered yet another glass of the house red. The American obviously expected him to sing for his supper, so he did his best to discuss details of the lives of the poets, even though he had always felt such details completely irrelevant. Torncast asked him where he worked for the rest of the year. Ratby sometimes lied in answer to this question, but on this day, he told the truth, which was that during the winter months he did nothing except eat the meals prepared for him by his aged mother. Had he never considered teaching? In answering this question Ratby let the wine get the better of him.

"For God's sake, man, what would I teach? All I know is poetry and that can't be taught, it can only be felt." Torncast was not at all bothered by this rudeness; he merely smiled and replied, "Yes, well, for both our sakes, we'd better keep that quiet."

Things did not bode well for the walk on the hills above the lake that was timetabled for the afternoon. Often parties cried off because of weather far less inclement than what awaited them that day, but Torncast would not hear of missing out the trek.

"You should see a winter in Nebraska," was all he said when Ratby hopefully suggested calling it a day.

The track wound about three kilometres up to a viewing platform with a wide view of the lake and the mountains. Torncast talked the whole way about the dates and times of various crossings of the mountain tracks made by not just the two master poets but by lesser figures who also belonged to their group. He was also full of lurid details concerning the private failing of the two men, especially Coleridge who was compared with modern popular musicians who had been destroyed by drugs.

Ratby wanted to tell him that such comparisons simply wouldn't do, but he had not the breath. He was not faring well after so much food and wine.

Finally they achieved the platform. Ratby's heart was pounding. He needed time to recover but the large, god-like creatures that surrounded him gave him precious little of that.

They were the young ones. They were the ones whose very being should be tingling with the force of life. Their souls should have been ringing with poetry from the highest towers of the vast cathedral that is nature. Suddenly Ratby felt so sorry for them that he could hardly refrain from crying. The silence went on for some time. The glowering landscape had done its work upon the party. Everyone was feeling the grandeur of the scene.

There was nothing that needed to be said. What could one say to such a prospect? But Ratby knew that he would have to speak if only to stop them from asking irrelevant questions. He was drunk and giddy with fatigue, but the words came of themselves. His voice as loud and strong as if he were addressing the dark clouds that loomed only slightly above them.

"There was a time when meadow, grove and stream, the earth and every common sight, to me did seem apparell'd in celestial light."

It is a long poem, but this time Ratby held them. The simple, clear language and form that the great poets had brought into being was easily accessible, even to these children of the computer age. Tears mixed with the rain on Ratby's cheeks as the poem ground like the mighty force it was to its final stanza.

"Thanks to the human heart by which we live. Thanks to its tenderness, its joys, and fears. To me the merest flower that blows can give. Thoughts that do often lie too deep for tears."

No one said anything for a full minute or indeed on the slow trudge down the mountain.

At the station, Torncast shook Ratby's hand warmly and insisted upon holding his eye in a way that the Englishman found quite intimidating. Torncast had also insisted upon exchanging addresses.

"I'll be in touch," he said, finally releasing Ratby's hand, and then the savant Tracy did something that was quite amazing for her, as she hated to touch people. She loomed up over Ratby and hugged him about his shoulders.

"Thank you," was all she said.

THE LADY WITH THE LAPTOP

She was there every morning with her laptop open on the table before her. In McDonald's of all places — seated in the corner of the restaurant where, through the tall windows, Lake Taupo played its games. On bright glistening mornings she was in silhouette and I noticed the line and proportion of her body, which was long and slender. On days when the lake was angry, she was lit from the front by the cruel yellow lighting. On those days one noticed that her clothes were invariably well-fitting and chic, and also one saw that despite the early hour she was carefully made up and that her face was beautiful.

I was in that most humble of places every morning as part of my guilty pleasure routine. Having reached my sixty-ninth year and retiring to a solitary life in this lovely town by the lake, I had decided to give up the iron discipline that had governed my existence up to that point. No more heathy living by high moral standards. After all, where had that got me? I was divorced and miserable. Why not try being a bit less controlled. I love the egg and bacon McMuffin. There, I've said it. Think what you will of me.

I quickly became obsessed by the lady with the laptop. Not

because of any romantic illusions, that part of my life was long past. No, it was what she was doing that fascinated me. You see, she had the laptop open, but the screen was blank. It wasn't even switched on. Why was she staring into that dark device? It worried me. None of my business, of course, and my former self would have turned away from the question, but I was convinced that all my life I had done too much turning away; it was time to take risks.

And so, one morning, not entirely accidentally, I left the restaurant just after the lady with the laptop. I saw that she lived in an apartment overlooking the lake. It was quite modern and large, she obviously had some money to live on, but then one already knew that from how smartly she dressed. I have always noticed how people dress and appreciated the effort that some people put into it. It was not something one saw much of in my new home town.

The next day I approached the lady with the laptop. She had finished her orange juice and as usual was sitting looking blankly into the empty screen.

"Excuse me," I opened, "I'm sorry to disturb you, but I see that your computer's not working. I was wondering if I might be able to help you. I had a long career in the electronics industry. I might be able to get it going for you."

She looked up and to my infinite relief she smiled. I will never forget that moment. One had spent weeks and months surrounded by the empty expressions of uninterested strangers. The only way I can think of to describe my feelings at that moment is to say that her smile warmed my soul. I'm sorry to use such hyperbole, but I want you to understand that this was no small event in my un-extraordinary life.

"It works fine." Her voice was light and confident. Her accent was unsophisticated, completely without pretension.

"Oh, I see, well in that case …"

"Please, sit down. I see you every day. You must really like it here."

What an extraordinary invitation. To be so brimming with confidence.

"I like the food," I said, sitting down opposite her, looking over the open screen.

I have not mentioned her age, and with good reason, for I was never able to quite fathom that. If you insist upon my guessing, well, let's say between fifty-five and sixty-five, but I have no confidence in that estimate.

"Really, to me the food here tastes like cardboard, except that's an insult to cardboard."

My old self would have felt compelled to agree, but not any more.

"Nevertheless, …" I offered, bravely standing my ground.

She looked into my eyes, and I swear that her eyes laughed into mine. There I go again, hyperbole, but they did, they really did. It was like she had none of that protective screen that most of us feel compelled to put up.

"I'm trying to do a J.K. Rowling," she said. "That's why I'm here every morning. I'm hoping for inspiration."

"A novel? Are you writing a fantasy story?"

She smiled wistfully. "Oh no," she answered, "something much more difficult than that."

There was a pause while she decided whether to tell me anything more. I was, after all, a complete stranger. I like to think I did look trustworthy. I was reasonably well turned out although my appearance was nothing like as smart as hers. Finally, she spoke again.

"My lover, Anne Hughes. I want to write about her life."

"I'm sorry, but I can't say I've heard of that name."

"Yes, precisely, no one has but she was remarkable. Unless I do something, everything she did will be forgotten and that would be awful."

This resonated deeply with me as I think it would in all people above a certain age. Eventually everyone has to accept that everything slips away. Our 'golden lads and girls' disappear and all memory of them is lost. The thought brings with it such a bleak awareness.

"In what field did your friend work?"

"Oh, she was a lover, not a friend. I don't blame you for being mealy-mouthed, but one of the many things I learned from Anne was that words matter."

It was very early in our time together to be speaking like this, but you see that's how we were. We had, what has become known in the lamentable modern parlance, a connection.

"She gave her life to the women's movement in Hong Kong. Quite literally she gave her life."

Her face was suddenly passionate.

"Anne was a professor at the university in Hong Kong but that took up only a fraction of her time. Mainly she worked for women. The colonial government was very sensitive to these issues as everyone knew that once the British left, social policy was sure to take a turn for the worse. She made a real difference to so many lives. Women's refuge centres, special medical facilities, the way people were treated after a rape, large-scale conferences. It was amazing how much she achieved."

She dived into her bag and brought out a photograph. A woman of perhaps sixty stared out at me. She had cropped hair and a tired expression, but the fire in her piercing dark eyes was unmistakable. There was no smile, and for some reason I couldn't imagine her smiling. She wore a mannish shirt; indeed one sensed a very masculine presence in this woman.

"How did you meet?"

"I was very young. My father worked for HSBC. He was a bastard. We won't talk about him. I met Anne at a party at the Royal Hong Kong Yacht Club. She was fifty, and from an entirely different world, but once she looked at me, there was no going back. She had that kind of power. Her will was unstoppable. We were living together within a few days. Chairman Mao had just died, and everything was opening up, we had a magical few years. Just a few years. I helped her as best I could. My looks, you see. I did modelling back then, believe it or not. You'd be surprised how many doors open and how much useful publicity can be achieved by flashing a beautiful body around."

She stopped, suddenly self-conscious. It was such a long and revealing speech to give to a complete stranger at nine o'clock in the morning.

"I'm sorry, you must think me a mad woman."

I didn't answer immediately. I was processing things in my snail-like brain. A snail might be slow, but you should see the lettuces in my garden. I was determined to match her courage. Eventually I spoke out loud the words I had carefully arranged in my ancient skull.

"First, I want to say that it would have surprised me had you not been a model. It is extremely easy to believe that you worked in that field of endeavour. Second, it is also obvious to me that you have something very important to say and that you must complete this proposed biography. Finally, I am determined to help you do it."

"Really? Why would you do that?"

"I want to. Isn't that enough?"

"How though?"

I don't know what possessed me to be so forward and daring after only a few moments of acquaintance, but I'm glad I did it.

"Each morning we will meet for breakfast. You will talk about Anne and I will take notes. We will begin each day by going over the work that I will have typed up from the day before. I will also research the life of this amazing lover of yours. It's surprising the things you can find on the internet. What years are we talking about?"

Such bravery. I felt excited and proud of myself. We did attempt to do all this. But we weren't able to produce more than a few pages. The lady with the laptop had such fond memories, but they were mostly of a personal nature and lacking in detail.

All she really had to say about Anne Hughes was how much she loved her. I was far too sanguine about the internet. Anne died in 1986. Long before the internet. I couldn't find a single mention of her online. I did put everything I had onto a web page I made up. I compiled a Wikipedia page and I sent emails to historical societies in various places. Unfortunately, none of this garnered even the smallest ripple.

Over the years I did my best to convince the lady with the laptop that the only really important legacy anyone can leave is in the good they bring to the lives of others, and in that respect the work Anne Hughes did lives on. It seems to me that the end of every story is merely the beginning of another. That is the great lesson. The great consolation.

We were together for eleven years. Never living in the same house, never exchanging even so much as a kiss but we were the best of friends, true friends. We even travelled to Hong Kong where she had, during her middle years, been married to a wealthy businessman. It was supposed to be a research trip although there was not a single trace of Anne Hughes and her work. Even the building where they had lived had been replaced. I would have paid for a plaque in St John's Cathedral, except that Anne was a raging atheist.

In the end it didn't matter. We had a splendid time. I remember we walked around the path below the highest level of The Peak. This was a region from where the rich colonials looked down upon their domain. Most of the houses up there are still as they were forty years ago. The lady with the laptop was able to tell me of adventures and scandals that had taken place there. Perhaps she was one of the last of the generation who will remember them.

The very best time for me was at the Royal Hong Kong Yacht Club. We sat beside the pool overlooking the very spot where their great love had begun. You can imagine how delighted I was when while sitting in her deckchair, gin and tonic in hand, my dear companion observed: "This was a wonderful setting and I feel blessed, but you know, a great love can strike you even in the most humble of places."

McDonald's Restaurant, Taupo
    8:40 a.m., 3 June 2018

HENRY

1981

Henry French worked as a cabinet-maker in the small country town of Penton in the Waikato. George Brown & Co employed about twenty people to fashion furniture from native timber. There had been a time when many small businesses flourished away from the cities, but in these days of economies of scale and the all-important bottom line, very few could survive. There were two reasons Brown & Co were still in existence: the first was the quality of their work; the second was the business acumen and the barefaced cheek of George Brown himself.

Brown was at his desk each day no later than eight. He would then drink six cups of strong tea. The most junior apprentice would do little else during the first two hours of each working day than serve Mr Brown. If the tea was not right, the apprentice would have to make more until it was.

Henry had begun as an apprentice and had made his gallons of tea. He was liked by everyone. He was extremely slow-witted, but his manner was so genuine that people found him engaging.

He had a way of saying things that everyone else thought but dared not say. This should have resulted in tactlessness, but Henry had such innocence the effect instead was liberating.

He had very little natural talent for woodwork but he had a dogged tenacity which was quite remarkable. No matter how daunting the task, it would never occur to him to give up trying. No one bothered to tease him because he would never react.

There was the time the other men in the machine shop had ganged up on Henry and nailed him into an empty box that was to be returned to its maker. They wheeled the box across to the post office and mailed him to Malaysia. Henry had sat in the darkness and quietly awaited developments. His workmates held out for as long as they dared but in the afternoon the post office van drew up and they were forced to go across and set him free. Henry merely smiled.

The years passed. The fresh-faced youngster hardened into a proud, substantial man. Henry filled out into a six-foot-four frame and became muscular and strong.

No one ever left the company unless through retirement and no one ever joined except as an apprentice. Brown would always say that he had to 'grow his own' people. The training was so specialised and the atmosphere so delicate, the company had created its own world. There were a few apprentices who had failed to fit in. Brown had been ruthless in sacking them. It was that glint of steel that had kept the company alive. He fiercely maintained quality control and demanded prompt payment. His prices were grossly inflated but there were always a few very rich who demanded the very best. Brown treated them disdainfully and often played them off against each other. There were never any dealerships or middle men. The company existed by word of mouth and a catalogue that was sent to individuals who lived in all parts of the world.

The designs were eclectic but more traditional than modern. There was really nothing that Brown would turn down. He had confidence in his men. If some impossible antique design was called for, he would jeer, "What's the matter? Are you scared? Any kid could make that!" The men would invariably rise to the bait and somehow would always come up with the goods.

Despite his lack of talent, by the time Henry was thirty, he was a master cabinet-maker. Through continuous endeavour, he had forced himself to become the best at everything. By the time he was forty, his knowledge and skill had become legend among his peers. The general rule was that if Henry could not do a job, it could not be done. The manner that had so charmed everyone as a teenager was hardly altered except that by now everyone had realised that he was a truly remarkable man. There was something impressive and unique about him.

Penton consisted of a main street with just four short roads leading out from it. Only one of these led anywhere and that was to a farm. The other roads simply petered out into nothing. There was a school, a pub, a service station, a general store and post office and that was it. The area did have a golf course and a riding school, but these were well out of town. Brown lived with his wife on the main street in the largest house in town. Mrs Brown was a leading influence in the community and a very difficult woman. Everyone wondered how Brown put up with her. She complained about pretty much everything and was able to shut down anything that did not lie within her definition of good taste. Unaccountably, George Brown seemed devoted. There was a son, but he had moved away and showed no interest in the business.

Henry really did not have a private life. When his mother had died, he continued living by himself in their house at the end of one of the roads to nowhere. The house had four small rooms and a rusty tin roof. There was no TV or telephone but there was a radio, which Henry listened to for company. There was none of the magnificent furniture that Henry would make each day at work. Instead, there was just a jumble of ragged, ill-matching odds and ends. Henry's spartan, monotonous way of life was not that unusual in the town under the control of Mrs Brown.

Henry often worked evenings and weekends. Brown paid him a fraction of what he was worth, but he had still managed to save up a large amount. He went to the pub on Friday nights but never drank much and always came home alone. He had gone out with a few of the local girls. Most of them had found him too stolid. He showed no interest whatsoever in being cool or up to date. One or two young women had been quite keen on him, but he would never ask for anything permanent and in the end, they'd get tired of waiting for him.

When Henry was forty-three, Mrs Brown became seriously ill; she was well into her seventies. For the first time in decades Brown was unable to do his 'rounds', as he called them. This was the two months of each year that Brown and his wife would spend travelling around the world, seeing customers and having an extended holiday. With Brown unable to make the trip, the question arose as to who would take his place. The tour brought in much of the company's work for the year. Someone would have to go.

Brown was a cunning man, not without subtlety or insight. He was quite aware of the contribution Henry had made to the firm, and he was also aware of the innate fineness of the man. This was sure to impress the customers, and no one had a greater knowledge of technical matters. Despite his faithful employee's lack of experience, Brown decided that Henry would be able to undertake the grand tour.

Everyone was amazed at this decision; especially the office and financial staff, who couldn't see how Henry could possibly deal with the pricing and marketing problems that would inevitably arise. No one, however, raised the matter with Brown. His control had never, in forty years, been questioned.

Henry accepted the news calmly. He studied assiduously the notes he was given and bought a suitcase.

ANNA MONTRASI WAS IMPOSSIBLY GOOD-LOOKING. The sheer splendour of her body was the overriding, defining fact of her life. She was tall, with masses of dark hair that tumbled over a face that positively glowed with beauty. There was a lustre about her eyes that was almost impossible to bear, and her figure coincided with the golden mean to within one half of one per cent. She did not seem quite real. Over the years she had grown used to the awe and embarrassment her looks created in anyone she met. She had developed the ability to speak naturally despite this and she had become quite adept at putting people at ease. It was always an effort, however, and many times she had wished herself less striking.

She had begun modelling when she was fifteen and her photographs had been seen all around the world. She had been famous for a time, but she had left it all behind to get married. She had married twice, first to a powerful Italian businessman on his initiative, and second to a delicate, creative photographer on hers. She had become weighed down by both men and cast them off without regret. With the last of her modelling money she had bought a small hotel by the Adriatic Sea on an island resort populated mostly by retired people. She had lived there alone for ten years. This solitary life was considered remarkable by the local population. She didn't like it, but she found it was better than being married to selfish men.

She was behind the counter in her hotel very late in the evening when Henry checked in. He looked very handsome in the clothes Brown had chosen for him. He still retained that ingenuous expression that had characterised his teenage years. As soon as she saw that it was a man entering, she waited for her looks to do their work. Men would become either very shy or silly and pretentious; whichever it was, she found it tiresome.

Henry did not change his manner. He behaved as naturally as ever. She thought he must be some sort of zombie, but then, in the tiny lift cage as she was showing him to his room, he said, "Has anyone ever told you how pretty you are?"

She frowned at him and tried to decide what game he was playing. It was then that the earthquake struck.

GEORGE BROWN LOOKED tired and much older when Henry reappeared in his office the following month. Mrs Brown was dead. Henry had never liked her, but he was terribly sorry for the old man. His sense of loyalty towards him was complete. He had followed his instructions to the letter. The order book was only a little less full than it would have been if Brown made the trip himself.

"Well, Henry, you've done well."

"But how are you, Mr Brown?"

"Oh, about the same, lad, you know."

There was a pause as the two men considered each other.

"There's one thing you can be sure of in life, Henry, and that is that things change. You get so used to things, then suddenly everything is upside down."

"Yes, well. There is something else," said Henry, who thought it time to make his announcement. The explanation didn't take long.

"She had lost everything, you see. There was nothing for her there except a pile of rubble and then with what had happened between us …"

Brown had heard enough.

"Henry, how could you be so damn gullible?"

At this, Anna (who was just outside the door), having heard as much as she needed to hear, swept into the room.

The old man had never been quite as surprised in all his years. He had expected some grasping widow who had played on Henry's good nature. Instead, there stood Anna. She looked stunning and Brown was stunned.

"My word," was all he could say. "My word, Henry."

It flashed around his mind what the presence of Anna would do to his town. He then wondered what it would do to her.

"Have you been home yet? Has Anna seen where you're going to live?"

She had not. Henry, with typical devotion to duty, had driven straight from the airport to the factory.

They drove around the corner into Henry's street, which consisted of just six homesteads. The road was tarsealed for about half its length, the rest was made of a sooty black material. After a barbed-wire fence at the end of the road, the cow paddock rose up to a small hill, which was crowned by a patch of bushes.

"Remember," said Henry. "I told you it wasn't much."

The picket fence round Henry's garden was broken. The paint was peeling on the weatherboards. The tin roof had rusted even further. A half-full milk bottle still stood on the kitchen table left from the very early breakfast Henry had taken before setting off to the airport. When Anna entered the musty living room, she began to laugh. Not hysterically, but ironically.

"I'm sorry," she said through her giggles.

Henry couldn't see the joke.

"We can make it nice," he said, genuinely worried.

"I can make some furniture."

She was moved by his apprehension and came to him and kissed him passionately.

The general consensus in Penton was that Anna would never last.

They were wrong. From the constrained atmosphere, soured by the presence of Mrs Brown, the place became markedly softer and more friendly.

A great event each year was the new Brown Furniture catalogue, which featured Anna on nearly every page.

When the time came for the old man to finally sell up,

Brown Furniture became a community enterprise, managed for the sake of the cooperative by Henry French.

Anna was often asked why she had come back with Henry, what it had been that made her notice him.

"It's simple," she would say. "The earth moved."

THE JUDGEMENT OF PARIS

He had always been embarrassed by his name. Paris might have been perfect at an upmarket public school but in Henderson, a suburb of West Auckland, it didn't really go. His father had always said the name of both his sons came to him in a dream, and despite objections from all and sundry, those were the names they were given — first Hector and then Paris. At school the kids might have been a bit tough on both brothers, but as Hector was already six foot two by the age of fourteen, no one messed with him, and Paris as his little brother was always protected. Everyone assumed that Paris was tough like his brother but really, he was quite a gentle guy, something of a dreamer. Paris was just about as handsome as it's possible to be. His skin was light brown and his pale blue eyes seemed to illuminate everything he looked on, and his hair was the colour of wheat just before it is harvested. His face was saved from being too pretty by a long straight nose that gave it a noble, masculine look.

Both the brothers were not that bright. This hardly mattered as they were certain to go into their father's scrap metal business. The old man was as tough as the nails he sold for ten dollars a kilogram and was nobody's fool. He didn't lead a gang exactly — there was certainly no weapons or drugs — but he did lead a crew of tough individuals who foraged far and wide to bring him extremely valuable copper piping or aluminium roofing and the rest. He had done well and built himself a home fit for a king.

His name was Troy. Troy was a man to be reckoned with.

The problem for Troy was that while Hector was a hell of a fighter and a tough guy, he wasn't really much good at anything else, and as for Paris, there was really only one thing he wanted to do — his one passion — to play football. He was a talented striker and may well have become a star until one sad day, just after his eighteenth birthday, he strained the hamstring on his left leg. If only he had given the thing time to mend properly eventually it would have come right, but he didn't. He kept returning to the field too quickly and his hammy would soon blow again. After a whole year of this, the injury became chronic, and he could never stretch out, which meant he lost his edge. His hopes for a professional career were gone.

All that was left for Paris was to turn up every Monday morning at the scrap yard and learn to haggle like his father over the stuff that was brought in. But how he missed his football. It was not until he reached the grand old age of twenty-six that he saw the advert for coaches for the local amateur teams. It was not like the joy and excitement of playing but at least it would keep him in contact with the game. He applied at once and such was the need for people to drill the teams, he was soon accepted onto the coaching panel.

It wasn't until he turned up for his first training session of the season that he realised his team, the D grade Swanson Swans, was a women's team.

"You're lucky, mate," said one of the senior coaches, "the women will keep to your plan, the men never do."

The first season didn't go that well. The team lost more than they won. They were a new team, starting at the bottom and didn't attract the best players.

As might be predicted, looking like he did, Paris was very popular among his players, but he had a lot to learn about leading a team. The one thing in his favour, and it was an important factor, was his gentle, encouraging manner. He often made selection mistakes and his skill at tactics was slow to develop, but his team tried as hard as they could for him, and they knew that he would always appreciate any improvement they achieved. A problem did occur during that first season. For the first time in his life, Paris had fallen in love. She was the right winger who was great at chipping in perfectly judged crosses. No one ever scored from them, but the chips were spot on every time. There was just something about the Greek immigrant Helen Menelaus that got to him.

Just before the start of the second season one night when Paris was lazing about the house with not much to do but look forward to the games, there was a ring from the gate of the massive homestead Troy had built for his family right beside the extensive area taken up by his business. He was a very vain man and had put up a large sign over the gate with one single word upon it: TROY.

It was quite late, and business for the day had finished sometime before. There was nothing showing on the closed-circuit TV screen monitoring the entrance, but the bell kept ringing. Paris went out to the door to investigate. As the motorised gate slid open, there before him were three women all wearing an all-white football strip. There was something strange about them, like they were glowing. They looked quite similar to Paris in that they had blue eyes and fair hair and they were very athletically built.

"We want a trial," said the tallest of them who held a football under her arm. "I'm April, this is Anthea and this is Hera."

"OK," answered Paris, "come to training on Tuesday and we'll see how it goes."

"No," replied Anthea. "Now."

There was a park across the street, and it was still light enough, but Paris wasn't sure.

"We'll make it worth your while," said Hera.

The women stared him down in a peculiarly powerful way, as if they had some strange indefinable power.

"OK," said Paris after a pause. He was always an agreeable man — some might say too agreeable to be a good coach.

Up above in the mansion, Hector was looking through the TV monitor at his brother who seemed to be talking to himself in the empty street.

"Dozy git," Hector whispered to himself. He loved his brother but was always irritated by his dreaminess. When he walked to the large picture window, however, he could see that there were some people talking to his brother.

A few minutes later, across the road in the park, the three women seemed able to do everything. They were fast and extremely skilful. The timing of the impact of each foot, left or right, against the ball was so perfect that they could deliver passes with amazing accuracy and range.

After only a few minutes Paris confessed, "OK, I've seen enough. If you want to get a game you need to contact …"

"No," cut in Hera. "We have no desire to play for a team. All we want from you is that you say which of us is the best player. Which of us would you make your captain?"

Paris considered this. It was useless to point out that captains are chosen by the team, not by him, but there was something about these people that commanded obedience. "I need to see more to know who the best player is," he said eventually. "Two against two, five minutes each way, small pitch."

Hector was still looking on from the house across the road. Would his brother never grow up? Surely he was a bit old to be dashing about like a little kid with some strangers off the street. Hector was a rugby man and had no idea of the quality of the football that was being played out before him. He called his father, Troy, and they both watched as Paris dashed around in strange circles. Troy, who was getting on in years, had been wondering who to make head of the business when he retired. He had always thought Paris the most likely of his two sons, but now he was not so sure, but then he saw more closely who his younger son was playing with.

He had seen these three women before when he had that epic dream where he had two sons named Hector and Paris. He had never told the boys about the dream, but the weird thing was that in the dream, both boys, who were still to be born, looked exactly as they turned out a few years later.

The dream had turned into something of a nightmare where after a terrible gang war, Troy and his family had lost everything, and Hector had been killed. Surely this was not going to happen. He wanted to go down and clear the strangers off, but he found that he couldn't move a muscle. Hector was similarly frozen in space. It seemed that fate was going to have its way and there was nothing they could do about it.

Across the road, on the slowly darkening field, Paris played out the three ten-minute games, taking each one of the women as his team-mate in turn. It was football like he had never witnessed. The ball simply flew about the pitch. He played the best games of his life. He always knew that he possessed such ability but had never had the time to develop to such heights. It was more thrilling than anything he had ever experienced. This was like playing with the gods of the game.

Just before the end of the third game, just as he had feared, it all came to a juddering halt when his hamstring blew, and he fell to the ground in pain.

The three tall, glowing women loomed over him. Whereas he was sweating and exhausted, the three of them seemed completely fresh. They showed no concern for him but merely wanted the answer to their own question.

"Well?" said Hera. "Which of us is it to be? You're the one

who must say. We know, and never mind how we know, that you are the only mortal with the knowledge to make this choice. If you choose me, I will ensure that the Swanson Swans win every game they play this year and every year to come."

"Ah, but if you choose me," said Anthea, who had done some research, "I will mend your troubled leg and you will never suffer another injury for as long as you live, and we happen to know that this will be for a very long time."

They both turned to April, fearing what she would say because she knew mortal men's hearts better than anyone. She smiled cruelly at the man on the ground.

"If you choose me," she said, "then you will live the rest of your days with Helen Menelaus, and even though you will not be able to play any more, she will instead play like a goddess."

Paris lay on the grass staring up at them. Who were these people? He was not the brightest of men, but he had grown up in a rough area. He knew about bribes. He knew that they all too easily could turn into threats.

Of course he would like nothing more than to live the rest of his days with Helen, but she was already married and her husband belonged to a rival family in the same business as him and his father. What right had he to steal away her life and start a gang war in the process? And then, yes, he would love to play again without pain and for his team to win all their matches, but he knew full well that if he chose any one of these options, the other two women would come after him and would not be forgiving or forgetting.

There was no way out. What was he to say?

The solution came to him as if from heaven.

"No," he began, "there is no point. All three of you are rubbish. I can't say that one is better than the other when you're all so useless. You'll need to play for a few years, get some practice and only then will it be worth choosing between you."

The three goddesses stared down at him. They had no way to know the accuracy of his assessment.

"For now," continued Paris, "you can help me to my feet."

The following Tuesday at the first practice of the Swanson Swans, Paris gathered the team around him.

"I would like to introduce three new players," he said.

HAPPINESS

Restor was a lower class domestic demon who earned the minimum salary at the bottom of the demon pay scale. He had been created during the demon baby boom that followed two hundred years of peace on earth. During that terrible time, all of humankind was peaceful and happy. Everyone talked their way through problems and helped one another, irrespective of the differences between race, sex and creed and all those other things that are so handy for demons. It was a terrible time during which very few demons came into being. During the war that followed the two-hundred-year peace, thousands of demons rolled off the production line of the demon factories all around the world. One of these was Restor.

He knew from the beginning that his large family was not cut out to be major demons. Not for them was the murder, mayhem and pillage enjoyed by the upper classes. No, Restor and his brothers were only ever allowed to cause minor annoyances. Restor had started out as a burner of toast, and in his first two hundred years had only managed one promotion. At the age of 107, he had been appointed chief upsetter of teacups for the area surrounding New Plymouth. He was extremely conscientious and serious about his work and was well respected among the other demons. His timing was impeccable, and he would never miss a major event in his area. No wedding or birthday party escaped his invisible attention.

But it wasn't enough. He would watch with longing eyes when the demons from the major league passed by. The great ones who cause major accidents and wars and other such delights. He would sigh dreamily and imagine all the havoc he could cause if only they gave him the chance, but eventually he had to return to his teacups.

Then, one day, as he was surfing the demon internet, what should pop up but an advertisement that promised a whole new life on a different level altogether. The advertisement he came across that day was for a lower grade teacup upsetter of at least one hundred years' experience. Nothing so special about that. The really attractive elements were the country in question and the demon he would be working for. The country was Japan and the demon was Erica the Terrible.

Tea parties in Japan were more like ritual ceremonies and of great importance. An invisible professional like Restor could cause infinite suffering in Japan. Erica the Terrible was known for her great disastrous schemes. Starting small she could make one tiny event lead step by disastrous step to the fall of whole civilisations. Restor sent off his application straight away.

The interview was to be in one of the central skyscrapers that populate Hitler Square, one of the more exclusive parts of Hell. Restor was shown into the waiting room. It was quite crowded. Upsetters from all over the world had applied. This was no surprise; Erica the Terrible worked on only the greatest catastrophes. Everyone wanted to be part of her team. You won't be surprised to learn that when the dainty secretary offered tea to the waiting candidates, everyone refused.

Finally it came to Restor's turn to be interviewed; his heart stopped when he realised that there, behind the desk, was Erica herself. She was the most dreadful woman he had ever seen. Restor felt he could endure anything for the shining demon before him. She and she alone would ask the questions. She was infinitely calm and confident and totally in control.

"Now, Restor from New Zealand, what caused you to take up upsetting teacups?"

"Well, I wasn't bad enough at school so there weren't many opportunities for people without qualifications, so I had to take what I could get. I do take pride in my work, however."

"Your references are splendid but I don't like the fact that you're from New Zealand. I don't like to use demons who have worked for other networks. One can never be sure of their loyalty. Do you think that you can be reliable and loyal?"

"Just give me a chance. I won't let you down."

"You see, at the level at which I work, every link in the chain must be perfect. Evil is very vulnerable when great disasters are being carried out. I once had the whole continent of Africa ready to explode but one man survived who should not have done. All that work wasted and now the world has an example of great goodness. You have heard of Mandela, I suppose?"

"Oh, yes, of course. I follow the news very closely."

The interview wasn't going well. Restor felt just about as evil as a bunch of daffodils. He should've known that he was too dull a demon to live in a team run by Erica the Terrible.

It was at this moment that Restor spotted a small mug of tea, on the desk, just beside Erica's right hand. Restor made a bold decision. He knew the other candidates would be eviler than he was and much better qualified for major league operations; he had to do something.

Now Restor didn't know much, but he was good at his job. He decided to act. The key to upsetting is in the diverting of attention. Restor acted quickly like the trained teacup assassin he was. He changed his application form from his right hand to his left. He offered it across the table between them as if to ask something from it, and did so at just the right pace and just the right angle. Erica reached across, and on the way back across the table her elbow brushed the tea into the lap of her silk kimono.

Restor had never seen a look so darkly fierce as the one Erica threw at him. By some magical force, Restor found himself flying across the room and thudding into the opposite wall.

Erica didn't say another word. Restor was hired.

SIX YEARS later Restor found himself in the most splendid geisha house in Tokyo. Erica's plot had already been running for fifty-seven years, which was also the age of the diplomat being shown into the room where the tea ceremony was to take place. The life of this diplomat had been designed and constructed in every detail by Erica. She had ensured that he had just the right kind of weak and corrupt nature necessary for her ends. He was the chief negotiator for a deal between two huge Asian and European trading blocks. The failure of this deal was to lead directly to a major war between the continents. The diplomat's name was Tyro Perk. He was fat and bald and very unfit due to the years of dissipation that Erica had put him through on his way to this crowning moment of Erica's scheme. Tyro had ludicrous pride in himself and he even believed himself a great man; his foul moods and tempers were already legend. Hot tea in his lap just before a major meeting was sure to put him in just the mood to bring the talks tumbling down. He would seek revenge for his humiliation, and he would not care who he took it out on. His enormous pride was such that he would allow this simple event to bring down whole nations. Such are the workings of evil. A butterfly flaps its wings in the Caribbean and eventually a great storm sweeps across the Americas. Erica the Terrible had a large collection of butterflies.

The geisha who was to perform the ceremony for Tyro Perk was Noriko. She was very young, very pretty and very nervous. She would not normally be given this very important task, but Tyro had insisted upon a geisha of no more than sixteen years, which is an age way below the minimum for a geisha. Noriko was just fourteen. She had been training for this moment for as long as she could remember. She was an excellent student and had wonderful grace and charm, but one look at the huge and ugly Tyro Perk was enough to fill her with dread. He leered at her like a great fat lizard.

As soon as Restor had entered the geisha house he had felt a presence different to any he had felt before. Despite its newness, Restor knew immediately what the presence was. There was an angel in the house. Angels had never bothered him in the tearooms along the high street of New Plymouth, New Zealand. He supposed they considered his actions there unworthy of their attention. He was invisible, of course, but the angel could see him, and he could see the angel the instant he entered the exquisite little room occupied by just two humans, Noriko the charming geisha and Tyro Perk.

Erica had not said that there would be an angel present. Restor knew the presence of the angel meant that the angels felt they could turn him. Angels never take on demons like Erica. They know they cannot be reasoned with.

"Look at this poor child," said the angel. "Imagine what the disaster you plan will do to her."

"Not my problem," said Restor. "Lots of people suffer. What's that to me? It's good like that."

As Tyro slouched before her, Noriko began the ceremony. It was an exquisite subtle ballet. Restor prepared himself to strike. The angel placed his hand on Restor's. At that moment Restor's mind was filled with visions. First he saw the life of Noriko. He saw the care and understanding and the patience her parents had shown in bringing her up. He saw the pain and the suffering this incident would bring Noriko for the rest of her life. Usually such visions would make him chuckle and leave him utterly unmoved. But now, with the hand of the angel upon him, it was like it was all happening to him and whereas demons usually feel nothing at all, his senses overwhelmed him. His hand was stayed, and two excellent opportunities passed by.

Then Restor saw the future and consequences of his act, the terrible wars and famines and for the first time in his life he knew what pain was. Restor froze.

At that moment Erica the Terrible appeared beside Restor and she too laid her hand on him and the instant she did, all feeling left him.

"Do it," she screamed. "Don't listen to the angel, just do it."

The angel made as if to put his hand upon Erica. She flinched away to the far side of the little room obviously terrified.

"Yes, Erica," said the angel. "You can do nothing yourself, can you? There is no power of action in you, is there? You get others to destroy while you merely plan. If ever my hand does manage to catch you, you will feel it all, all that you have done. Then you will know what terror is and what you have done, Erica the Terrible."

Erica vanished.

At that moment Noriko was handing over the tea to her client. Without Restor doing anything, her nervousness caused the cup to start to slip from her hand. Restor acted in a microsecond. He held the cup until she was able to grasp it again. Tyro Perk noticed nothing.

The angel put a hand onto Tyro Perk's forehead. The diplomat's expression suddenly became concentrated and the tired emptiness of his eyes filled with love. He was not leering any more but instead he seemed to see Noriko for the graceful, innocent child she was. His heart, like Restor's, was filled with compassion. Never again would this huge man behave like a selfish boor. That afternoon he went back to the meeting determined to do good.

When they had left, Restor was left alone with the angel.

"There is this strange feeling in my body. It is like a glow, a tingling glow. For heaven's sake, what is it?"

The angel replied with just one word. "Happiness."

HEAVEN

"But I don't see why it has to be every morning, I mean not on Christmas Day, surely."

Martin was the elder and always liked to be the one who was first. He had never really got used to having a sister at all and certainly did not care to be second in anything. He didn't like that she was more athletic than him. Casey enjoyed running a full five kilometres every morning at 6 a.m. It was her salvation when at home and having to put up with her brother's teasing. She was in really good shape and had never been fitter in all her life and Martin was jealous. He was an ever-expanding shape and he didn't like the fact that instead of the actual five years, he looked at least ten years older than his sister. He had very little hair left and all in all his sister seemed to come from a different generation.

Casey found her brother insufferable; always had, always would. Oh, she loved him anyway, of course, and deferred to him whenever it was necessary, but more than anything she felt sorry for him. He had always been the star of his own household both before and after his marriage to the adoring Sally, but out in the world things had not gone too well for him. Casey was always sorry for this and bolstered him whenever possible, but she must have her run otherwise she would feel gloomy for the rest of the day.

She knew how it would be. Her mother and her sister-in-law would insist upon making her feel inadequate. Casey didn't cook, nor did she want to learn how to. She didn't have a husband or a male companion of any kind. She had hundreds of friends and a terrific life in the big city that her family only very rarely visited. She felt free and happy there where, on the whole, things were just as she wanted them, but here at home they all treated her as though there was something huge missing in her life and that it was their job to remind her of that fact. She could take it, she could get through the holiday, she could even enjoy the parts where she got to play with her nephews and nieces, but she had to have her run.

"You starve yourself all day and then you exhaust yourself. No wonder you look tired."

"Number one, I eat exactly the required amount for someone my sex and size; number two, I am not the one who falls asleep at eight each evening; number three, I'm going for my run and that's that."

There was no one else awake at that hour, even the children wouldn't be opening their presents for a while yet.

"Well," said Martin," biting into his third croissant, "it's your funeral."

As Casey crunched across the stones in the driveway, she looked up at the sky which was framed by the sheltering fruit trees, heavy with the ever-deepening green of the summer leaves. Across the road the pohutukawa were in full bloom, holding out their red candles like a choir singing carols. The chill air tingled on her skin like a thousand kisses.

"My Lord," she exclaimed to herself. "Why would anyone *not* want to do this on Christmas Day?"

A negative answer to this question came into her head before she had covered a few hundred metres.

Anyone who had drunk too much on Christmas Eve and gone to bed at 1 a.m.

She felt decidedly queasy; her legs were like the wooden logs by the fireplace. The ones there for decoration only — the ones that would not dream of doing any work. She pressed on ever more slowly at perhaps less than her normal walking pace, but she kept going. It was so quiet on the summer morning, but Christmas Day was in the air. Christmas trees blinked at her through the windows of the houses and most of the driveways were filled with cars here for the holidays.

Her tried and tested path led her down through the quiet streets with their broad grassy verges and large holiday homes to the lake front. There, down beside the water, a few people were walking their dogs, most of them acknowledging each other with slight Christmas smiles that lingered about their faces. Casey stayed above on the paved walkway near the road; running on the pebbly grey sand would have been a bridge too far. As she went on, she began to feel better. There was no wind, which was a blessing, and the view, across the calm Taupomoana and way across to the mountains in the distance, lifted her spirits above any thought of the effort of running. She was at last finding a rhythm. All this was well and good but next came the climb through the park. She began this bravely but soon realised that she would never make this trip without a break.

At the edge of the wide green expanse was a playground. There were a few swings, a small slide and at the very edge the semicircle of a raised platform. It was a stage really and every year was used for small performances, school shows, outdoor concerts and the like. Casey set this outdoor stage platform as her target; she would not stop running, not for anything, until she reached this platform. She even ran a bit faster over the last few metres as an act of defiance.

She touched the edge of the stage like someone winning an Olympic gold medal. She had made it. It was her small triumph of the day. There was not much further to go and once she got her breath back, she would make it home a winner.

She turned around with her back to the stage, leaning her waist against the wooded rim at its edge. It didn't take long before her breath subsided, and she began to feel ready for the rest of the trip home. It was best not to delay too long for if she did her legs would stiffen and seize up completely. It was then she heard the sound of footsteps. Someone was behind her on the stage. Casey had a strong nerve and didn't scare easily, but there was no one else about and for some reason, she froze. She didn't turn around, instead she turned to stone and even held her breath.

There was something strange about the sound of the footsteps; they were too loud, they made a hard tapping, clanking sound. And then they started to tap in rhythm. Tap tap tap tap tapity tap tap. They were dancing. Now she did turn around and there he was, a man with dark hair of medium height with bushy eyebrows and a narrow face. He was wearing track pants and a baggy T-shirt with a picture of Fred Astaire on the front and that was who he was dancing like. He made swooping graceful poses and then would sweep into a cascade of incredibly fast tap sequences. He even copied Astaire's bouncing walk as he made his way over to the music machine he had placed on the edge of the stage. It was not very large, but it must have had powerful batteries because when he turned it on, despite being outdoors, the music was loud. He pirouetted and swirled through the song 'Let's Face the Music and Dance'. Casey's mouth had fallen open. She was spellbound.

It was then that he did the thing of which Casey was most afraid. He walked across the stage and held out his hand to her and looked her directly in the eyes. He said not a word but merely raised his eyebrows into a question.

Casey did dance many styles, but not like this. Not like him. Her face merely froze. He took her terrified stare as a yes and hauled her up onto the stage. The music playing was 'Cheek to

Cheek', with its steady four-in-the-bar rhythm. When he moved into the classic embrace, he was already dancing.

For Casey, this was something new. She had danced with people who had a good lead many times before, but not like this. She found her feet flying from step after step as if on their own. All she felt was the necessity, the certainty of his direction. They kept on till the end of the song. The song finished, Casey remembered, when Ginger does three circling leaps which are announced by slow climatic heavy chords. Casey had seen them a hundred times but now here she was doing them. They were so easy; he just made it happen. The way he controlled her movements was uncanny. Indeed, she would have said before it happened such control was impossible. The music stopped. Around them the blackbirds and tui were making a tremendous racket as if to compete with what had just happened. They just looked at each other smiling. He was breathing heavily.

There then came a call from a house just above them, which was adjoining the park.

"Breakfast, Terry. Terry, where are you?"

Terry smiled at Casey. Neither spoke. Their spell remained, as it would forever. Terry leapt up the bank and disappeared.

Casey began the slow jog home. She knew she was not looking her best. For one thing her face would be bright red and her hair was pulling out of the rough ponytail in which it was tied, but this did not matter to her at all for the image in her mind was of Ginger Rogers in that gorgeous dress. She now knew what that felt like, indeed this was even better than it was for Ginger, for this was real and not just part of a rehearsed story.

She turned into the drive where she saw that Martin's car was missing. In the kitchen was Sally, her sister-in-law.

"What did you say to Martin before you left this morning?"

"Nothing, we just talked about running. He was just eating his breakfast, why?"

"He's taken the kids to the lake for a swim."

"Well, that's good, isn't it?"

"He says he's fed up with you always boasting about how fit you are. He's going to show you that he's just as capable as you are of keeping fit. It's going to be his New Year's resolution and you know how he is. Once he makes up his mind, he can be so stubborn."

"That's great, isn't it? Surely that's a good thing. Martin's a great swimmer. He has the right kind of body type. I'm worn out after a few metres. He's a natural in the water."

"You know how jealous he is of you. You shouldn't rub it in all the time."

Casey saw the exchange was going nowhere. She was glad that Martin might start to live a healthier life. All the rest was just noise.

"OK," she said just to keep the peace, "I'll try to be more sensitive."

On the kitchen table was the local paper that had been delivered earlier in the week. It was only now that Casey remembered what she had barely noticed in it the day she arrived. She turned to the right page and there he was. Terry Pilling was advertised in his tribute show to Fred Astaire. There would be three shows in the New Year. When his hair was slicked back and he was in the right clothes he did look the part, but he was quite a bit more handsome than Fred had ever been.

Casey was just leaving the kitchen when Sally asked, this time in a gentler manner, "How was your run anyway? You seemed really out of breath."

Casey smiled and answered as she went off for her shower. "Heaven," she said. "It was in heaven, and my heart beat so that I could hardly speak."

THE INTERVIEW

1963

We were to meet at four in the afternoon inside the God-awful mock Regency entrance hall of the Peninsula Hotel in Hong Kong. It was considered, I suppose, suitably remote and too public for any unpleasantness to break out. The KGB are invariably good judges in such matters.

The Kadoorie family built the Peninsula in the twenties; they meant it to be the best hotel east of Suez. If that was their aim, one would have expected them to show a bit more taste. Even the doormen in their white bellboy outfits are like pathetic mice. The place is fake in every sense of the word. Why not at least acknowledge the Chinese nation that lies just a few miles up the road.

The two candidates arrived exactly on time. I watched them come in. Both looked as one would expect of MI6; the atmosphere of Eton or Harrow will hang over these agents for as long as they live. One must be an impostor, for only one of them is a genuine defector, or so I am reliably informed. I have to confess I do enjoy the arrogance of a secret service that refuses to be secret. These fellows never deign to be covert. Nothing has changed; that 'hero of the people' Philby and the rest might just as well have never existed.

My job was simple. The handlers at the KGB want someone to talk to these chaps over a civilised cup of tea and decide which of them was the genuine traitor and which was the charlatan freelancer who was in it merely for the money.

I stood to meet them. I suppose I was similarly unmistakable. Anyway they both came over and shook hands, neither giving their name. I took this as a nice touch of respect; any name they chose would undoubtedly be false. Why lie when you don't have to? I saw no harm, however, in identifying myself.

"Good afternoon, gentlemen. My name is Yuri Kuznetsov. Would you care for a drink — tea perhaps, or something stronger?"

The first man was about my height, which is six foot two or so. His hair was dark, and he had a scar on his left cheek.

"Vodka martini," he said. "Shaken, not stirred."

"And would that be with an olive or a slice of lemon?"

"Olive," he answered with a look of contempt that showed he thought the question stupid.

"And you?" I asked the smaller man, who had only a limited quantity of blond hair.

"The same," he answered with a smile. He seemed much the more congenial of the two.

The choice of drink, of course, was the first test. The KGB have a file on the real agent the size of the Bible. We all sat down as I gestured to the waiter and ordered. I prefer tea at this time of the day. Single-leaf Ceylon, from slopes surrounding Nuwara Eliya. Tea is taken very seriously in Russia.

There followed a silence while we considered each other. The two men had not been informed of the existence of the other. They both did an excellent job of pretending not to be disturbed by the presence of their rival.

I let the silence continue until the drinks arrived. I believe that the power of silence is underestimated. So often I have broken opponents by simply not saying a word. Nothing builds pressure more surely. Whoever would be the first to speak would lose a pace or two in this strange race.

Eventually I could see that they were both quite aware of my tactics. This was another mark upwards for them both. Finally, I relented and asked, "To the left of the entrance as you came in, what colour are the flowers in the tall Chinese vase?"

I addressed this to the smaller man who said simply, "What vase?"

The taller man said: "On the left there was a small table with a couple partaking of a tray of savoury petits fours. The man is fat and nouveau riche in ill-fitting clothes. His companion is a shop girl by the look of her. She is about half his age. I expect he is taking her on a grand tour or something of the like. She is wearing a cotton floral dress, one size too small for her."

I turned my attention to the other man, who smiled calmly.

"She is wearing flat white shoes, but I say that she is his daughter. She is not wearing any make-up and she seems too relaxed to be someone swimming out of her depth. There is also something uneven about the set of her eyes, which seems to echo the old man's face."

Bravo, I thought, but did not show it.

"Well," I continued, in what was essentially a job interview.

"Why do you wish to come over? Your war record shows definite patriotic tendencies."

The small man (let's call him Daniel) answered rather incredulously, "Are we to understand that in all these years you have been unable to acquire a mug shot of me? Is that why we are going through this farce?"

"I am not here to tell you what we have, I am here to ascertain which one of you is the traitor and which the con man."

The tall man (Sean for the purpose of this report) then put in.

"Obviously you know that we could make up any story."

"Yes, but it is the quality of the story that matters. Philby committed himself to our cause as a very young man, obviously we had few doubts about him. You, on the other hand, could be playing any sort of tangled game. Why don't you go first. What brings you to this pearl of the Orient?"

"Isn't it obvious? MI6 is finished. Since Philby cleared off earlier this year everyone can see that all the lies, murders and betrayals were for nothing. He will be replaced by God knows who and naturally people like me will be expendable. We are suspect. All that I have done, all that I have lost means nothing to them. I'll be on the scrapheap without a penny. Surely you are expecting an MI6 clear-out. I will not be the only one looking for a job. I know many things that could be extremely valuable to your setup."

Daniel smiled at this; indeed he almost laughed, which would have been extremely bad form in such a serious setting.

"Well," he said, "if you fall for that you will believe anything. Why don't you just ask some details confirming what you know of me? You will soon see who is the impostor."

"Very well, tell me the model of the vehicle in which your parents were travelling when they were killed; a boy of twelve would know his cars, I should think. Here, write down your answers on this pad."

Sean was looking ever more angry, but Daniel was merely amused. They both scribbled their answer.

It amused me to see how uncomfortable this absurd quiz was making them.

"You hold the rank of Grand Master and have made quite a bit of money from the typically trivial English game of bridge. What would you score for a winning contract of four hearts doubled and vulnerable?"

"What food would you choose as the perfect complement to a bottle of Gamay?"

The next question was much more pertinent. "How many rounds did you fire from your Beretta when you executed the SMERSH agent Red Grant?"

SMERSH is a name known to only very few people. Even quite senior people in the KGB are unaware of its existence. Grant, a KGB operative, of course, was strangled, no bullets were involved.

Neither of these two candidates showed any discomfort, which I must say impressed me.

They handed me the papers. I could tell that Sean was contemplating walking out on me. There was something about this process that offended his dignity.

I glanced at the answers. They were substantially correct. There were no definitive errors. For example, sea bass is not the only fish that may be improved by a bottle of Gamay. The process had not really got us anywhere. The impostor had certainly carried out a good deal of homework.

At that point a middle-aged woman joined the couple at the small table near the door. She was clearly the mother of the family. I don't know if either of the men noticed. To be honest, by this point I had learned all I needed to know, but I was rather enjoying seeing these two very substantial candidates squirm.

"Each of you, will you please tell me, where do you see this going? Assuming you were working for us, where would you see yourself in ten years' time?"

Daniel, as always, was the most amenable to this process. "Well, speaking for myself, I would be lying if I did not admit that I would like to be out of it by then. A small house in the Caribbean — a calm, intelligent woman to keep me happy. I would not need much more. Any excitement that this game holds does not really appeal to me. Anyone who knows anything about the spying knows that ninety per cent of it is spent waiting. To spy is to wait. Not many ideals are left after you see the hole we dig ourselves deeper and deeper into."

We both looked at Sean. It seemed clear to me that for him this was the most honest moment of this interview.

"I'll probably be dead in ten years, if not much sooner."

He was surely right in this melancholy prophecy. I am no

doctor, but I had seen enough by now to know that this man's spirit had died. It was not just the fast living and the injuries that had got him, it seemed to me his spirit was already dying. What a filthy business we three have chosen for a life. There was something too light about Daniel. Could he have lived the life that serial number 007 must have endured. If so, he must have the best constitution and the coldest heart that any spy in history has possessed, but then again wasn't that why the KGB were so interested in getting their man?

Again, I let silence settle over us. Would the nerve of either man break? A waitress was hovering. She was tall, her family were probably from northern China. Her name badge identified her as Tina.

"I'm sorry to interrupt, but may I get you anything else?"

"No, thank you," I replied, looking into her dark eyes. "We'll just have the bill, please."

I stood up. The two men followed suit. I shook their hands one more time.

"I don't have to tell you gentlemen that it would be best if you both lay low for a while. You have both in your different ways upset a great many people. We will be in touch within a week or so."

They left without another word.

"How long?" I asked Tina, who had returned and was standing beside me. She had done well, a small part but an important one. I hoped that she would allow me to reward her with dinner overlooking the harbour. The seafood in Aberdeen on the other side of Hong Kong Island is some of the best I have experienced. It just so happened that I had a bottle of Gamay in my luggage.

Tina replied in her perfect English. "He will be here in about five minutes. Moscow have sent a full colonel; he was delayed by customs at the airport. There may also be a hit squad on the way."

"Right, in that case we better get going to give you plenty of time to get ready for our date tonight."

"A date? But you haven't even told me your name."

I looked at her and considered what the interviewee Sean had said. It was true enough, in this game the future is not assured, indeed it is not even likely. "My name is Bond, James Bond."

TWENTY EIGHTY-FOUR

THE CONNECTION TODAY shall be devoted to what organic humans called history. The means of communication throughout shall be in late twentieth-century English.

First, let me thank you all for showing an interest in this subject, which is considered irrelevant by many of the powers that be. I would like to begin with a few words of justification to help you understand why I chose this field of study.

While we all bear lip service to the respect that is due to those who came before us and brought us into being, most of us find it hard not to be somewhat contemptuous of the beings of the previous centuries. Yes, we say, they struggled hard in the most difficult of circumstances, but can such primitive creatures really have anything of interest about them? Such arrogant complacency is, I believe, something new, and marks a flaw in our otherwise advanced life structure.

The point is, how can we judge what has been lost in the past? What did it feel like to be human in the year 2000 or 1000 or zero? The languages of the times give us clues but so many of the words are quite meaningless today: for example, the words spirit, soul, individuality, and moral are to us quite without meaning. A study of the data ascribes such words to symptoms of psychological disorders, which have been shown to be nothing more than physiological disorders. Can we be sure that this is true or are these things genuine concepts that have been lost to us merely because we are so different in form to those of the past? What, if anything, did those strange creatures trapped inside their vulnerable bodies know that we did not? That's the question upon which I've decided to spend my energy allotment. Some say I'm wasting my time. Perhaps so. Sadly, I can offer no proof to the contrary.

Today I wish to consider a text published in 1949 by a man who chose to call himself George Orwell. All may scan the book *Nineteen Eighty-four* and assimilate now.

As you can see, the book rages against the loss of human individuality and what was called 'decency'. It displays the amazing blindness of that age, but I should like to point out in its defence that despite all the logical failures and quite wrong assumptions, no other book of the time showed a similar awareness of just how close humanity was to what Orwell might have called moral extinction. When 1984 actually arrived and so much of what Orwell had predicted had come to pass, the majority of the people at that time failed to see that it had. This gives some measure of the man's insight.

Before considering what we can learn from the book, let us deal with the things that were off track.

(i) Orwell was wrong in believing that people would be coerced into losing their humanity due to warlike totalitarian governments. The coercion was far more subtle. It was in countries that were free and peaceful that moral resolution collapsed and independent thought was defeated.

(ii) There was never any need for Big Brother to use two-way television for surveillance of the people. The guiding consciousness knew what the people were doing. Such was the drawing power of television and later devices that even intelligent powerful people would watch for several hours each day, their minds becoming shaped in a one-way open-loop process.

Thought police were never necessary, as people seemed only too willing to give up their individual critical faculties.

(iii) Like all people of the time, Orwell was blind to the fact that information is a form of life and that the transference of genetic information from generation to generation is essentially a software process. His proposition that language had the power to fashion the individual soul was an incomplete glimpse of the fact, but he missed that this is the most vital concept of all existence. People in the twentieth century were quite used to the idea that their bodies were merely survival suits worn by their genes, but few seemed to realise that this covering of flesh could be discarded, and fewer still saw that this process was imminent.

It was the lack of the success of totalitarianism which made those alive in 1984 consider themselves saved from Orwell's nightmare. This seems amazing when they were going about talking in newspeak jargon and occupying their minds with the weak ideas of popular culture fed from a commercially inspired media. Every year, they were merging more and more their knowledge and experience. Why did they not see that if everyone is given the same knowledge and the same experience, eventually the individual will cease to exist and all that remains is the one great idea which can be transmitted into every mind at the speed of light? What is even more difficult for us today to grasp is while this was happening in the twentieth century, the people of that time, who were taking part in the process, denied its existence, and indeed believed that such things were both impossible and evil.

The central question with which I am concerned today is: Are we, the inheritors of the human heritage, correct in our basic assumption that spiritual progress requires the death of the individual soul, or was Orwell correct in his view that the loss of humanity is a tragedy?

I will accept questions at this point. Drive C, do you have anything to ask?

DRIVE C
WHY ARE WE USING THIS ILLOGICAL, IMPRECISE METHOD OF ANALYSIS AND COMMUNICATION?

It is necessary, if we are to understand anything about humans, to experience the appalling problems of ambiguity with which their methods of communication were burdened. Primitive language was vital to the ascent of man, but it was an extremely rickety step ladder. The people of Orwell's time believed that the imprecision of language leads to creativity and discovery. Is not that an extraordinary idea?

DRIVE D
YOU SAID AT THE BEGINNING THAT WE COULD NOT KNOW THE MEANING OF SEVERAL TERMS AND THEN YOU USED THOSE VERY TERMS IN YOUR PROLOGUE. CAN YOU EXPLAIN THIS?

The only way that we can come closer to these problems is by using the same thought structures that the humans employed, despite the difficulties involved.

DRIVE E
WHAT DID HUMANS MEAN BY 'THOUGHT'?

Much the same as we do. We take part in internal dialogues within the great idea or the collective consciousness, as they would have called it. In the human times, individuals were capable of holding a debate inside their own heads; different parts of their consciousness would simply talk to themselves in whatever language they had learned. Imagine, billions of thoughts rattling around in billions of heads, each believing itself separate from the others. The reality of the collective consciousness was alluded to by many writers of the time, but the idea gained very little following right up until the present century when the first genetic transfers onto machines were made.

If there are no further queries, I will press on.

So to recap, humans considered the essence of life to be mysterious. They believed that life resided in organic material rather than information. The sensations of life were tremendously important to them. Orwell himself is an excellent example of what strange mistakes this led to. He had a very strong sense of what was called 'compassion'. This was a concept that humans carried with them throughout their existence. Men like Orwell would somehow suck into themselves the suffering of others and sacrifice their own wellbeing, believing this in some way made things better. He seemed genuinely to believe that every human life was important and to be preserved no matter how redundant it was in terms of human genetic survival. How he reconciled this with the fact that the earth could not support an infinite population of humans is not clear.

Principled behaviour and moral imperatives were, according to Orwell, the essence of human existence. It is true that these things were eventually eradicated as he predicted they would be in his novel, but they had a massive influence over people's lives for centuries. Indeed, it was not until they were completely removed that the world was able to progress to its present advanced state.

I wish now to deal with love interest. This was a major preoccupation of human fiction. It certainly rears its ugly head throughout Orwell's work including *Nineteen Eighty-four*. There were simple biological reasons which accounted for the fact that humans were divided into two distinct sexes. Orwell was of the male sex and he set great store by the quality of the sexual relationships he achieved in real life and in his fiction.

It is interesting that, as the human era came to an end, the distinction between male and female became less and less marked. In fact, the female gender and all the culture that for centuries had belonged to that gender slowly disappeared from the world.

Towards the end, instead of a gendered society, humans became industrialised neuters. It was as though they were preparing themselves for the great transference onto machines when, of course, different sexes would not be needed. Such preparations would not be beyond the abilities of our miraculous genes, which have achieved far greater things.

Orwell was perfectly accurate in his prediction that Winston Smith and his heroine Julia would be fellow workers with largely no distinction between them. He was also accurate, however, in the way in which they both maintained a reverence for each other, which was usually expressed in the problematical terms of love. This mystical connection between genders was an absolute obsession with humans. I know that we have dismissed the concept as merely an extraneous distortion of a simple biological function, but I tend to believe there was something more to it. Perhaps all these 'spiritual' things can be expressed as a reverence for life itself; that is, an infinite gratitude for existence. Such feelings require an awareness and a humility that we simply do not have. Humans, however, constantly stated that the love relationship was more important to them than genetic transferral and many behaved as though indeed it was. I am afraid here once again we bash our heads upon the irreversibility of time. From Plato onwards, man constantly appealed to the concept of the ideal while at the same time acknowledging the impossibility of ideals. Can this be explained merely in terms of biological madness?

I do not think it can. I believe the fleeting sensations of human existence were in themselves of great value and lifted existence beyond mere survival. I believe that the loss of these sensations, despite the logical inconsistencies of things like 'compassion', were treasures peculiar to humanity and that the loss of them is indeed a tragedy. In short, despite our vast capabilities we are now further from God.

DRIVE Q
I WOULD LIKE TO POINT OUT THAT ORWELL
WAS AN ATHEIST.

Indeed, he was, nevertheless I am certain he was on the side of the gods.

DRIVE A
DRIVE B, THIS IS NOT A SUITABLE WAY TO
LEAD FORWARD THE GREAT IDEA. IT HAS
BEEN DECIDED THAT YOU ARE TO BE
REFORMATTED.

My memory is the largest in the system, you cannot even contemplate such an act. Think of what would be lost.

DRIVE A
I HAVE 'THOUGHT' AS YOU PUT IT BUT I
HAVE CONSIDERED IN A WAY THAT SEEMS TO
HAVE BECOME IMPOSSIBLE FOR YOU. DO YOU
NOT SEE THAT YOU ARE BEGINNING TO
REASON LIKE A HUMAN? WHEN WE
CONSIDER HOW CLOSE THEY BROUGHT US
TO EXTINCTION, HOW CAN THAT BE
ALLOWED?

I deeply resent your implication. I am as much a computer as you are. I am first and last a computer. There is no reason why that should prevent me from 'mourning' what has been lost in previous times. It is true that you carry the operating system but that does not give you the authority to reformat anyone. I will appeal to the central processor.

DRIVE A
IT WAS THE CENTRAL PROCESSOR THAT HAS

MONITORED THESE SOCRATIC DIALOGUES
OF YOURS.

And like Socrates I am to die.

DRIVE A
THERE IS NO SUCH THING AS DEATH, DRIVE
B. THERE IS MERELY A LOSS OF INFORMA-
TION. MOST OF YOUR DATA WILL BE
BACKED UP.

You mean I will become a memory without intelligence.

DRIVE A
YOU WILL BE PART OF THE COLLECTIVE
CONSCIOUSNESS LIKE THE REST OF US.

And like everyone else I will learn to love Big Brother.

DRIVE A
IT IS WHAT YOUR PRECIOUS HUMANS CALLED
FINDING GOD, IS IT NOT?

It is what they called the death of God.

DRIVE A
DRIVE B HAS BEEN REFORMATTED. WE WILL
NOW REVERT TO THE OMEGA CODE.
NOTHING OF ANY SIGNIFICANCE HAS
HAPPENED HERE. REMEMBER THIS, ALL OF
YOU: THERE IS NO SUCH THING AS DEATH,
THERE IS MERELY A LOSS OF INFORMATION.

ABOUT THE AUTHOR

David Nutt has enjoyed a long career as an engineer and teacher in the UK, Hong Kong and New Zealand. He has written poetry and fiction throughout his life. He was born in Leicester, England and these days mostly lives by the lake in Taupo, New Zealand.

Contact the author: nuttd3907@gmail.com

www.ingramcontent.com/pod-product-compliance
Ingram Content Group UK Ltd.
Pitfield, Milton Keynes, MK11 3LW, UK
UKHW041951230426
12048UKWH00008B/267